Stro

MW01199974

With unusual secrets, she's left the big city behind as she follows her heart to Wishing Springs, Texas, for a simple life as the new owner of the Sweet Dreams Motel—she's looking for a simple life so the last thing she's expecting is the heart-knocking effect the handsome sheriff has on her.

Lara Strong needs a new beginning, and as a reader of the *Gotta Have Hope* newspaper column, she's drawn to this very special town. Her heart needs to heal to stay strong like her father, who was as tough as his name, always taught her before she lost him. Now, she is moving forward in her own way, buying the motel, living a quiet life, and helping customers feel the comfort of home while they visit. She'll touch their lives briefly, bringing satisfaction and healing to hers. *This* is the security she needs, only knowing her customers briefly and therefore feeling no pain when she watches them drive away.

Jake Morgan has a town to look out for, a ranch to keep up, and a heart to keep locked away. But the moment he meets Lara, something inside of him sparks to life. Something he's conflicted about but unable to deny. But sometimes, despite your strength, if love's got a hold on you, it's a hard thing to deny…and if the town is on the side with that love—two people fighting to stand their ground might just find that they've got to find hope in their heart's determination to open up to love each other.

Happily-ever-after is just a few heart-touching, eye-opening moments away, if Jake and Lara will give it a chance. Welcome back to Wishing Springs, Texas, where love happens, and the town cheers it on…and sometimes gives it a shove in the right direction.

STRONG LOVING COWBOY

A Gotta Have Hope, Book Four

DEBRA CLOPTON

STRONG LOVING COWBOY

Copyright © 2024 Debra Clopton Parks

CHAPTER ONE

Her heart thundering, intent on changing her life, Lara Strong drove her black convertible Porsche 911 into Wishing Springs, Texas. To help calm her nerves, the top was down, letting the breeze flow around her, helping keep her past from hanging on to her…

A past she loved and hated all in one thought.

Her past that gave her a happy life with her loving parents and then the past that stole them both away in an instant at the same time—her fingers instantly tightened on the steering wheel, reminding her to smile.

Driving gave her peace. Driving gave her wonderful memories of Lara and her dad checking out cars at an early age. And later too, this 911 had been his favorite of all of them, and it had been a reminder to him to relax in his sometimes stressful career. The 911 was now her reminder to do the same in her life without the two people she loved and lost.

This small, fast convertible was a reminder of them.

But she kept it also because she, like her dad, loved speed.

And that was part of why this convertible was her choice, because with the top down at sixty-five to seventy miles an hour, legal speed *faked* the feeling of a hundred miles an hour. A smile burst to her lips because she might like speed, but she'd been taught to take care of herself and that meant *not* going crazy in a car. But, a car that moved instantly when you pressed the gas could save your life. Same with a great brake to stop the car before disaster happened.

If only that could have worked in the private jet her parents had been in when they'd gone down.

Pushing those thoughts away, she focused on the small-town where she was intending to start a new life on her own terms. Terms that she controlled.

She loved reading the amazing *"Gotta Have Hope"* newspaper column published in the *Houston Tribune.*

The author, Maggie Hope Monahan, had recently told her readers that the Sweet Dreams Motel was now up for sale. Instantly, Lara had thrown her heart into making a bid that included money and a written letter to Pebble Hanover Radcliff. Adding Radcliff to her name and the owner Rand Radcliff to Pebble's life as her husband was now why the motel was for sale. Pebble wanted to choose the right person to leave her history with as she began her new life with her husband.

It was all so touching, the story that Maggie had quickly told her readers was about overcoming problems and sadness with hope and determination to be happy again. That was what Maggie's column was all about and so it was a perfect thing for her to showcase for her readers. Hope was always there. And because of that, here Lara was. The note she'd written, plus the bid, had gotten her the invite to meet Pebble.

Her story and need to overcome it had hopefully given her the chance of being the one Pebble chose to sell it too. She had no idea how many others were getting to meet Pebble.

She pressed her brake and stopped at the single

blinking red light on Main Street, knowing she'd take a left turn here and the Sweet Dreams Motel would be in sight. Her heart went into overdrive as she carefully turned left and eased across the space and then turned down the street that hopefully led to the place where she would begin her new life.

At least she prayed that it was.

As a reader, like many other Americans, she was an avid reader of Maggie's wonderful advice column. She'd been drawn to the town of Wishing Springs, where the column was written. The questions people mailed in to her were from all over the country, asking for Maggie's heartfelt words of advice, and her advice always touched Lara's heart. Sometimes there were even romances that she helped with, but that would not be something Lara would ever be worried about.

No, she read the advice column because of the way Maggie spoke of the town she loved. She always advised people to surround themselves with people that would help them and their community. Her articles were so wonderful in helping people with their questions about loss of love, finding love, and living life to its fullness while dealing with pains and troubles. And her answers always gave hope.

Lara had pain, but who didn't? But she strove to overcome it as her parents would have wanted her to, but it wasn't easy. She tried to focus on the fact that everyone had hardships, had lost someone close to them. But for the last year, she'd stayed hidden away in her spacious home, having learned not only that her mom and dad were gone but so was the man she'd thought she was falling in love with. She'd realized that the man, the wimp she thought she had a chance for a future with, was only trying to use *her* to get to her dad. Her dad and his money.

Now her money.

Her father had known what he was doing when he'd been raising her, teaching her what to watch out for, and she'd instantly squashed that relationship like a sledgehammer to a piece of cheese—the piece of sleaze had raced for cover. After all, she was her father's child, and in that moment, she'd been the strong woman her father had raised her to be. Had prepared her to be.

Her heart still hurt, but she'd started looking at her

options. Her own needs.

And here she was at her new start. A simpler life, a quiet life, and her note to Pebble that had won her this opportunity, told a portion of her story. About being the only family member left and needing a place to start her new life. A quiet place where she could help others as she found her way on her own.

Those words were what got her here, where Pebble was waiting on the right person, and she wanted to know that she was selling her beloved motel to the person who needed it. To the person who would give it her heart and carry on Pebble's love of the place and her legacy. And that was what Lara knew she was going to do.

If Pebble chose her. The moment she'd received the call from Pebble, she felt like an author who had been trying to sell her first book for twenty years and finally got the "Come meet me." She hadn't hesitated, and here she was. Pebble, the sweet lady, had finally married the love of her heart and was moving on. She had been blessed to have two men who she loved but lost the first one early, then finally let the second one into her aching heart, and they planned to travel some now that they were together.

That meant she was selling the third love of her life, her motel. She just had to find the right person. Now, she was meeting Pebble and prayed she would sell the motel to her but she'd already decided that even if she wasn't picked, this wonderful town was going to be her home now. She'd packed up, and when the truck came to town, it would either come here or to the home Lara would buy if Pebble didn't sell to her. This was her new beginning.

She pulled into the parking area that was surrounded by picturesque, colorful cabins. Her heart thundered as she put her 911 into park and turned off the perfect purring engine. Determined, she got out of the low-riding car and gently closed the door. Then she walked with determined steps to the motel office door that had a beautiful wreath of artificial roses welcoming her. She took a breath of air and then opened the door to the pleasant sound of a soft jingle announcing she was here.

A small, smiling lady hustled around the end of the check-in desk and met Lara near the door. "Lara, welcome to Wishing Springs. I am so very excited to meet you."

She hadn't even asked her name. Just assumed she was Lara. "I'm glad to be here."

"You're the only one I'm expecting today, so I just assume you are Lara." She filled in the sentence Lara had wondered about. She led the way into the office where there was a small desk, another computer, and sparkling light fixtures that put beautiful light into the room that had a warmth to it that she liked. There was also a beautiful rug on the floor. It was a small desk, but there were bookshelves and photos of what looked like maybe customers. She was attracted to the office, but it was the lovely white-haired lady who walked and sat behind her desk as she motioned for Lara to take the seat on the other side that really captured her attention.

She sank in to the seat, it was very comfortable. It was a soft white and blue cloth, and she sat very straight, keeping her back forward from the backrest and smiled at Pebble. "Thank you so much for inviting me here. I couldn't wait to drive into town."

"I am so thrilled that you came. I can tell you

everyone is looking forward to meeting you." Pebble rested her hands on the desk and beamed.

"I know that you haven't made a decision, but no matter what, I've decided to make Wishing Springs my home. As I said in my letter, I needed a new start, and I follow Maggie's articles. I like everything she says about this lovely place. But, no pressure." She laughed, "I'm just glad to be here."

Pebble's blue eyes twinkled. "Perfect. I just had to meet you, had to see you and make sure you are real. I felt your emotions as I read your note and just needed to know my feelings were right. You have not disappointed me. The day me and my first husband bought this place, I was home. It was a little dream of wanting people to feel welcome and special. I got a lot of letters, but your letter stood out because it was so close to my own feelings. And now that I've met you, it's a done deal. The paperwork will just take a little bit and then I'll hand the keys and the title to you. So welcome to my world."

Lara was overwhelmed by her words. "That quick?" she gasped. "It's mine? Honestly, I have no words except thank you. I am thrilled to be able to step in, and as I promised in the letter, I'll carry on this legacy that you've left here. I can't wait to make people feel welcome here. And I'm looking forward to meeting everyone. I feel like I already know them."

Pebble stood up came around the desk and wrapped her arms around her, giving her a warm, tight hug. "Darling, I'm thrilled you're here too, and guess what? We're going to The Bull Barn for lunch. Believe me, there are people waiting to meet you, and I promised them that if you accepted my offer, then we would be there to celebrate."

"I can't wait." She took a deep breath closed her eyes, and tilted her head back to thank the good Lord that He had given her this blessing. Then she opened her eyes to find sweet Pebble smiling.

"*He's* listening. And that is all we need."

Lara nodded. God had made a path for her after the pit of sorrow she'd been in this year after losing her parents. And the coniving man she'd thought she cared for…could love, and been so wrong. So, maybe her decision to find a new life being satisfied to touch lives without being seen was the right move. It felt right to her, and right now, that was what she would go with.

* * *

Jake Morgan, the sheriff of Wishing Springs, held The Bull Barn door open for one of his good friends. "It's been a good year for your family."

Champion quarter horse trainer, Tru Monahan, walked in, then waited for Jake to step in beside him. "You're right." He grinned. "*Real* good for our family. Me, Bo, and Jarrod all now have wives and babies, Pops has no worries about losing his ranch any longer, and *you* helped us stop the cattle rustlers. So, yeah, we're all happy and that makes Pops even happier."

Jake knew how much that meant to his friends. They'd saved their ranch from the destructive abuse of their dad, who had a secret gambling habit none of them knew about until after he and their mother died in a private plane crash.

Jake had watched the Monahan brothers work hard to regain control of the ranch that they would've lost because of the dad's horrible secret. They'd worked so hard because their Pops, before his Alzheimer's, had worked harder winning championships, training champion quarter horses, and building the amazing Four of Hearts Ranch for his grandsons. They'd almost lost it but had won that fight, but they were slowly losing Pops and were grateful for every moment he was with them. In good mind or wandering mind, Pops meant so much to them.

Tru had been driven to keep his heritage by winning on the champion cutting horses he'd raised and trained like Pops had taught him. And now, Tru was a proud husband and father as were his brothers, and Jake knew helped Pops smile more than ever.

"It's great to see all of y'all happy. It's amazing actually." He glanced around the dining room just as Big Shorty, the owner, came hustling from the swinging doors of the kitchen.

"Okay, you two fellas, come on in. It's going to be a busy lunch rush, but there's a few tables available. I'm going to put y'all over here." He led the way to a table on the far side of the diner.

Jake scanned the room, nodding at people who acknowledged him. They had voted him in and hadn't yet voted him out, and for that he was grateful. He loved his job. His gaze landed on a very pretty woman sitting at the table next to the one Shorty was headed toward.

She was surrounded by the ladies of the town— Pebble Howard Radcliff, the newlywed and owner of the Sweet Dreams Motel. Claire Lyn Conway and Reba Moorsby, the owners of the Cut Up And Roll hair salon. All three great friends were instigators sometimes and a rescue team other times—but always a never-ending cheering section for the town.

His gaze barely took them in though, since it was instantly pulled back to the side view of the woman sitting with them. She hadn't even glanced toward them as they were walking toward their table, yet he wanted her to look his way. It was an odd "want" for him, the cowboy with an iron grip on his heart. He had a town to keep safe and a lot of ranches to keep safe. The idea of getting mixed up in a romance like his buddies had done might not have a happy ending. Why had one look at this lady had him thinking this?

The pain of his mother when she'd lost his dad plagued him and how much she'd hated it when he'd followed in his dad's footsteps and became a sheriff too. That had him relooking at the women he'd been attracted to and he'd pulled back and refocused on his job. He hadn't been out on a date in a long time. But there was no denying that something about this lady struck him like a sledgehammer.

"Jake and Tru, come on over here and meet Lara Strong," Clara Lyn declared, waving her hand, her mass of bracelets chiming and bringing him back to reality.

Shorty had placed their menus on their table. "I'll get y'all some tea," he said, hitching a bushy brow at Jake as he passed by him.

Jake had a funny feeling that this was not an accident that Shorty had picked this table. He realized too that he was just standing there as the attractive lady turned her head their way.

Tru held his hand out to her. "I'm Tru Monahan and glad to meet you, Lara."

"She is our new motel owner," Reba declared. "She's buying Pebbles' place."

"That's great." Tru looked at Pebble as he let go of Lara's hand. "So now you and Rand can be free to see the world." He grinned.

"Yes, we are," Pebble said, as pink rose to her cheeks. "Though we love our town, we do want to travel some."

Tru looked at him and Jake realized that it was his turn to welcome their new town member. His gaze locked with hers, and he lifted his hand and forced himself to speak. "I'm Sheriff Jake Morgan. Welcome to our town."

She hesitated, her gaze locking on his before she placed her hand in his. Lighting struck like a bomb in that instant, blasting through him like nothing he'd ever felt. Her eyes flashed as if she too had felt it.

What had just happened? He forced himself to speak, "I'll be making sure you stay safe there at the motel—just like I do or did for Miss Pebble. Making sure no one comes in and gives you a hard time. Making sure everyone who comes to rent a room knows you have security."

"He's really good at his job, our sheriff," Clara Lyn

said, grinning at him.

Reba huffed. "He's a workaholic though and he doesn't date."

He saw Lara's teal blue eyes darken. He glanced at Pebble and saw she had a look on her face that was a little unusual as did Reba and Clara Lyn. Their looks made him feel off. He looked back at Lara, who looked off-kilter too.

"Thank you, Sheriff," she said firmly. "That's good to know there is someone looking out after my business. But, you can let go of my hand now."

Only then did he realize he was still holding her hand. He dropped it, realizing that was what everyone had been looking at. Sheriff Morgan, infatuated with their new motel owner.

He stepped back. "If you need me—for *help* or bad customers, the number is there in the office and Pebble can show you." He felt off-balanced with what had just happened. "When do you take over?" There, he sounded more normal.

"Everything is out of my apartment," Pebble said. "So, she can move in whenever she wants to. She already said she was going to move here even if I didn't sell the motel to her."

"Really," Tru said, finally talking again. "I thought this was an interview, from what Maggie said."

Pebble smiled brilliantly. "That's what it was. I just needed to see her, talk to her, and make sure she was sincere in that letter of hers. And I could tell instantly that she was who I wanted to sell to. So, we will be signing papers after lunch, and my sweet Rand will be there with me. Then for the first time in a very long time, I will be without my sweet motel. But, though I'm sad, I have a great feeling about it. She'd come to Wishing Springs to stay one way or the other even if I didn't sell to her."

She'd come to live here with or without buying the motel. Interesting. "Do you read Maggie's column?" Jake asked.

"Doesn't everyone?" she said, smiling at Tru. "Your wife is amazing."

It was true, but, now he knew, she was here looking for love and he wasn't interested in that at all. He had business to tend to—he had a town to keep safe. He had ranches to keep watch on besides the town and people he loved to watch out for, and that was his responsibility. Making a wrong move in his life—his love life hadn't been a mistake he was willing to make. The idea of taking that chance and it not having a happy ending was his main roadblock.

So, he didn't take those chances but there was no denying that something about the lady sitting there at the table hit him like a sledge hammer.

CHAPTER TWO

Lara hoped the strange feelings that just looking at the handsome sheriff sent through her were a reaction to what she'd thought was excellent meatloaf, but was now wondering if it was bad meatloaf, and she was reacting. Feeling queasy she watched—tried not to watch—as he headed toward his chair at the table too close to hers. His tall, lean body looking strong—

She yanked her gaze away from watching him and found the ladies all had very odd expressions radiating from their faces. *What?* "I-I'm about to be a resident of this town and that thrills me," she blurted out, desperate to get her oddly shaking insides to calm down.

Clara Lyn chuckled, lifted her hand, bracelets jingling as she patted Lara's shoulder. "You're already a resident. We've welcomed you and now a great welcome from those two." She nodded her head toward Sheriff Jake and Tru. "And now you get to meet these two funny brothers."

Two older, identical men walked up to stand beside their table. Both grinned crooked grins—thankfully they had on different shirts, one was red polka dot, one was red stripes.

"Hi, Doonie and Doobie, it's good to meet you. I'm Lara and I read Maggie's articles so they don't even have to tell me who you are."

Red Polka Dot held out his hand. "Well, little lady, I am Doonie, and this is Doobie. So today, remember red polka dots is Doonie and stripes is Doobie."

She grinned as Doobie held out his hand, "Nice to meet *you*. And just so you know if you're not sure if he's me or I'm him, know *everyone* gets us confused so no worries, we're completely used to it."

"It's great to meet you, Doobie and Doonie, I'm about to buy Pebble's Sweet Dreams Motel, and I'm going to work *really* hard to figure out who is who. I think there has to be something different, some *tiny* difference somewhere."

The brothers looked at each other, hitched their eyebrows, then looked back at her in unison. Together they said, "Good luck." Then they headed toward the exit.

Reba chuckled. "Yes, good luck. Those two we never know about, and if anyone figures out who is who, they just don't let on."

Did Reba know the difference?

Bracelets rattling, Clara Lyn waved her hand. "Those two entertain us, switching out. Sometimes they even share being the mayor. If we have figured it out, we don't let on. That would ruin the fun of these two thinking they have us fooled."

They *did* know which was which. That intrigued her even more. A town that let two identical twins get by with having fun with them. "So they share the role as the mayor of the town?"

Pebble's smile widened. "Yes, if one has something else to do, the other goes to the meetings as the mayor."

Lara laughed, her hand spanned over her heart. What fun she was going to have. And then she leaned forward a little and her gaze slid to the table next to theirs to find Sheriff Jake Morgan watching her.

* * *

Jake got in his truck after saying goodbye to Tru, who was heading to see what his wife had just texted him about. Tru had a grin on his face as he headed for his truck, his destination on his mind. Jake walked to his truck trying not to envy that Tru had someone waiting to see him at home.

He was glad for all of his friends, especially the Monahan men, as they were like family to him. They'd gone to school together, and he had watched them all find love and now he was watching their families growing with babies. And they loved it. Pops did too. Jake pushed away the envy that suddenly filled him. They'd watched him lose his dad when he was in high school, and they knew, like everyone in town knew, how the loss had affected his mother. More so when he'd chosen to follow in his dad's footsteps. And then to protect her, because she was afraid of losing him or his future wife going through what she'd gone through, he wasn't getting married. And that meant not having children. She wasn't getting grandchildren but she was fine with that, she didn't want to watch them grow up without their father.

Not that he was planning on dying in the line of duty, but his dad hadn't planned on it either. He'd been helping someone on the side of the road and would have done that whether he was a lawman or a cowboy. Like Jake, he was a protector. Like his dad he had a strong, protective overture and he put others in place of himself. Especially his mother. But…it had never felt as off-based as it did right now.

He got into his official sheriff's SUV, it reminded him where his mind should be, not where it was. He cranked the powerful engine with a hard twist to the key, pulled the gear shift in place a little rougher than needed, he'd backed like he always did making it easy to head out quickly when needed. Now, his foot remained on the brake as the convertible black Porsche drew his attention like the lady who drove it was sparking trouble in his mind. He stepped on the gas then pulled forward slowly, carefully.

Movement drew his gaze to the door of The Bull, as he shortened the name in his convoluted brain. Then the lady on his mind, causing problems, stepped onto the porch. Their gazes locked even with the window glass and fifteen feet between them. As he always did when passing people, he automatically tipped his hat. She turned away, practically spun away, and he drove out of the parking lot, door closed on any ideas his brain was trying to make feasible. Like a punch in the jaw, her turning away said it all, *keep away*.

He rubbed his jaw as he drove, having needed the punch because his crazy mind was still trying to go out of bounds to a path he had no plans to travel down. And he wasn't happy that one look at the new lady in town had given him this—longing?

He shut that down and drove to the office, got out of the truck, and met one of his deputies at the door.

Deputy Kevin Colten tipped his hat as he paused on the sidewalk. "Sir, Brad Ross found a dead cow, killed he thinks by something big. He says he thinks it could have been a cougar. You and I both know they're hidden ghosts moving across all the country they travel without being seen much."

Jake nodded, totally agreeing. "Yes, they have a way of being a shadow. And we are in a path of at least one. The Buckley brothers spotted one near their ranch on the outskirts of Lone Star, Texas, where they live. I went there and helped hunt for it because it was roaming close to a bed and breakfast. We didn't find it, and it didn't attack anyone before moving on."

"They travel a huge ratio of land. We are in a hundred-mile radius of Lone Star. So it could be the same animal."

Jake hitched a corner of his lips up. "You've been doing your research. Good work. Let me know what you figure out."

"Yes, sir."

Kevin headed for his car and Jake headed into his office. He had a great staff of deputies to watch out for the town. In his office, he sank into his chair, placed his palms flat on the desktop, and took a breath. He loved his job, protecting this town from harm. Just like his dad, Sheriff Chad Morgan, had done until he'd died while helping a family fix a tire on a dark night, and a drunk had slammed into him and killed him.

His dad had been the sheriff before him and died in the line of duty—not shot but looking out for people. In his heart, standing there during the funeral, Jake had known he was going to take up the call to follow in his dad's footsteps. He'd had other plans, but Jake had taken up his mission to protect this town, and he'd gotten the right training and, then he'd come back to town and was where he was supposed to be.

He just did it alone. Because his sweet mom had gone through torture losing his dad, her husband. His dad had believed in insurance in case something happened to him and this had enabled his mom to run away. She now lived in Florida in a safe place for women who lived alone but liked to enjoy themselves. She'd needed help doing that but had found a way by surrounding herself with ladies who had nothing to do but play tennis, golf, and whatever else they wanted to do…hide or runaway. He pushed that intruding thought away. She'd earned her life by loving a man who'd given his life, and he would never judge her for not wanting to face that again.

He talked to her regularly, but she never asked him about his job. He let it go because he knew she worried that one day, like his dad, she would lose him too. He didn't plan on that. He was very careful to not let his guard down, even when he was helping someone fix a flat at any time of day.

He prayed one day maybe his mother would find new love, his dad would have

wanted that. His dad had been dead since he was seventeen and on the varsity football team. He'd been on the field when he'd gotten the call and his life had never been the same since then.

Everyone respected his dad but they didn't talk with him about it, knowing how hard it was on him. His father's deputies had taken on the "upholding the law" for Wishing Springs until he'd returned prepared and ready.

And they'd never see him leave office until they kicked him out. But he also took his life seriously, and he'd seen how losing his dad had hurt his mom, and he was conflicted about taking a wife—if he ever found someone he couldn't resist—he shut down that thought. If he fell in love with someone, loved her so deeply that he couldn't push her away, that meant he might put her in the position his mother had been in and now lived with. He knew he could never cause that kind of pain to someone he loved. He had been at peace with that, so why now was it pushing at him?

Exasperated, he yanked his hands from the desk, pushed his chair back with his booted feet, and stood. It was time to get to work. He'd learned all those years ago to push this all to the back of his mind and not dwell on it. But that new lady in town had struck him like a slash of a whip. She was dazzling with her quiet look, her sparkling eyes, and a determined don't-come-near-me look. That too reminded him of his mom. She'd gotten that look after losing his dad. He would never take the chance of falling in love with a woman and causing her pain like that.

That meant no thinking about the pretty lady with the serious closed-look in her eyes who had just taken over the Sweet Dreams Motel. There would never be sweet dreams for him when it came to falling in love.

CHAPTER THREE

Lara sat at her desk, *her* desk. She had come straight back to the motel after signing papers at the lawyer's office with two happy people watching. The wonderful man, Rand Radcliff, as small as he was, had hugged her first, then spun and swept Pebble into a heartfelt hug. Lara sighed watching, knowing love at any age could be wonderful. If you chose to go down that path.

She was choosing a different path as the proud owner of the Sweet Dreams Motel. And that gave her the opportunity to quietly watch for where she could help people. This motel could give her *her* dreams now.

The motel wasn't busy all the time, yes when they held town-involved things, Pebble had told her it would be very busy. But she'd bought it knowing that it wasn't a huge money maker and she didn't need it to be. She just needed a place that gave her something to do and a purpose. Something she enjoyed and a place to just to be still and watch for her time and places to give.

This week it was closed because Pebble had already planned a weekend getaway so it was a great week to have Lara come and buy, if it worked out, which it did. It would also, if she bought it, give her a week to get settled in. Pebble thought things out and that was for certain.

There were bookings for the next week and weekend because the town was having its very well-loved gathering, people had booked early for the event they loved in May. She wasn't really sure what the event was but would soon find out because there was a town meeting on Monday evening. And she would be there.

She had a new life now. A life not in New York, she was grateful not to be in the city any longer. She'd grown up there, because of her father's amazing mind with building businesses. He was in the business of making huge money while helping others. He had even prepared for his death by helping her cash out of many things automatically upon his death to free her up from stress but leaving her advice on choosing how she wanted to live and use the money. She sighed, thinking about it. Yes, she had worked for her dad but couldn't and didn't want to continue in that large office and city without him. She now had to step out and find her own life.

His last words in his will touched her. "I'm gone so now, step out and do things your way. Find your life and enjoy it while helping others as you choose." If she'd been younger she wouldn't have really understood that her life with her parents had been different than most. But she was an adult. Was a shy, internal thinker who hadn't thought she was different. But she was.

The Monahan brothers had lost their parents in a plane crash that revealed their dad wasn't who they'd believed. Her father and mother's deaths had only revealed how much they loved her and not lied to her. They'd left a lot to her, so much…but also had donated a lot, and for that she was grateful. But even from the grave her father was telling her to trust herself but not to stress out.

And so, she was trying to disappear quietly into the shadows of a small town that would let her be herself.

Now, she picked up the main key to the rooms and headed out the door. Right now, she was going on a tour of her new motel. Pebble had given her blessing on any changes she wanted to make, it was now hers. She smiled as she went out the door and headed to see her place.

The sun was shining brightly, just the way she was. She was in Texas, where the sun shone almost all the time. Even in December, January, and February—yes, they had their cold days but then they got relief with a not so cold day. Today it was a great summer day, and that was the kind of day she loved the most.

She opened the first door of room one and stepped inside halfway expecting to find a bag of cookies greeting her. Pebble made homemade cookies that greeted each guest, but she was closed for the week, so there were no cookies waiting as a welcome. Lara *loved* to bake and would continue this tradition. Her sweet mother loved to cook, had loved, she'd lost her too, but this would be her way of remembering so many wonderful moments spent with her mother in the kitchen before joining her father in the office.

In between cooking and traveling with her parents, there were times when she had to be home with her nanny. A very nice lady, her dad had made sure she was, but also his making sure Lara could take care of herself had started young, because she'd almost been kidnapped as a four year old. So, he'd prepared her to take care of herself if he'd made a mistake and she or anyone wasn't who they said they were. He took the time and had prepared her for when he wasn't around. She could take care of herself very well, quiet or shy didn't matter. She had a black belt and a self-defense education. She was a *Strong*, and her dad had made sure it was more than her last name. And for that she was grateful even though she hadn't understood early on why he put her in all those trainings. Now she understood.

He'd always said when the trainers came in that if something happened to him or when he wasn't around, he'd wanted her to be able to fight.

So yes, she was quiet but she was a fighter.

Pushing the thoughts away, she smiled at the room, her pounding heart calming. The room was lovely and she breathed a sigh. Here, in this small town, she had no fears of anything, even without her parents around. She could take care of herself...she could enjoy being behind the scenes. She could have peace. For some crazy reason her mind went instantly to the sheriff.

The handsome Sheriff Jake Morgan and thinking of him did not bring peace. It put her entire body on alert. There was something about that man that turned on every red alert inside of her, and there was no peace in that.

Avoid him. That was what she'd be doing. Absolutely staying out of his way.

* * *

The sunset was beginning, and like a golden diamond dropping slowly into ocean blue water on the horizon, it was going to be a memorable one...one to watch with someone special.

Jake pushed the thought away, and though he wasn't on duty and he trusted his deputies, driving around town before dusk was a hard to break habit. So here he was heading back to town after he'd gotten off four hours earlier and made the rounds on his ranch, fed his horses and cows, making a round through the pastures checking fences and relaxing. No relaxing today. His busy brain kept returning to The Bull Barn, and the pretty newcomer turning her back on him.

What was that about? Why was he stuck on that thought?

He had a town to take care of, and his ranch was supposed to be his place of relaxing and enjoying life...but lately it was just his place to be when there was nothing else to do. So, as he always did, he headed to town. It was nearing nine o'clock and most everything was closed by that time, even The Bull Barn. They would still be cleaning up because they closed at nine but everything else closed by five. He made his rounds, slow and steady, with open eyes, he drove through every street.

As he turned down the road that connected to Main

Street on the far end, the road that passed by Sweet Dreams Motel, he slowed, he always wanted to make sure everything was fine for Pebble. He surveyed the side that was first in view then eased on by the office that had always housed Pebble but now Lara. He saw the light outside the office on, and to his surprise, he saw the new owner sitting in the chair beside the table illuminated by the light above the door. His foot hit the brake and he pulled into the drive.

Nothing unusual about what he was doing. If it had been Pebble, he had always pulled in, got out, and sat down in the chair on the other side of the small table, and he and Pebble talked. They'd talk about her day and sometimes they talked about Rand, he was her husband now, her friend only for a long time. A friend with a problem and she and he both worried about him.

Alcohol was a dangerous drink and Rand had given in to it, but his love for Pebble and her love for him had helped him overcome his alcoholism and now they were married and happy.

Everyone was thrilled after they'd eloped and gotten married. Just the thought made him smile.

Pushing the smile away he pulled into the drive far enough past Lara that his lights weren't in her eyes. His passenger door was even with where she sat so he could have rolled it down and asked her how she was doing. But he didn't. No, he put it in park, turned off the engine, stepped out of the truck, and strode around the backend then stopped.

He tipped his hat. "Hi, I thought when I saw you sitting there, where I normally see Pebble, that I should stop. I usually stopped to check on her and see how her day went." It was true. "I hope you don't mind, but old habits die hard. *And* I need to stand by my promise to her request, making sure you're doing okay."

For a moment he wasn't sure she was going to speak, as she just sat there listening. Then she placed her hands on her pale blue, well-worn jean covered thighs as a gentle but wary smile turned up her previously tense lips.

Relief rolled through him, calming his heart that was on a rampage.

"Thank you," she said, waving out toward the chair on the other side of the small table. "Please have a seat."

"Thanks." He removed his hat and then stepped forward and sat down in the wooden chair, propped an elbow on the wooden table between them ,placed his fingertips on the wood, and tapped. His habit, of when his mind was rolling, of tapping his fingertips on his thigh or a tabletop or the outside of his open truck window or whatever happened to be around took hold. He'd spent many hours in this chair over the years. Pebble was like an aunt to him after his dad's death and his mother needing to leave the town, and he enjoyed sitting here.

"It's been a great day," she continued, giving him a smile. "I bought the motel and met a lot of nice people today. I'm not the best at being the center of attention, but glad to be here."

She'd definitely been the center of attention and probably would remain there for a while. "Everyone is glad you're here. So, are you enjoying the evening? Settling in?"

"Yes. I have a few days to settle in, so I have time to come out here and relax. Pebble is a very smart lady, setting it up so guests won't arrive until next Friday.

Giving me a week to adjust to town and ownership. Pebble and Rand are going on a trip."

"Pebble is very smart and the town is overjoyed that she and Rand finally got married and are having fun. They'll be seeing the world and spending time together. But we're also glad our town remains their home base." His fingers tapped again, he stopped moments ago, but now they were going again.

"You're a thumper," she said, her lips lifted at the edges and her eyes twinkled in the light from the doorway.

She was beautiful—he yanked his hand from the table and placed it on his thigh. "Sorry, it is usually only when I'm alone in my truck or at my desk alone and contemplating…"

Lara's smile widened broadly, striking him in the heart like a lightning bolt. "My dad was a thumper too, when he was thinking. He had a brilliant brain and it worked constantly. I could always tell whenever I was approaching him by how fast he was tapping whether it was a good time to talk or to leave and let him think."

He grinned, couldn't help it, and relaxed a little.

"I'm that way when I have a lot on my mind. My fingers start moving on their own, sometimes fast and sometimes slow, depending on how my mind is contemplating my thoughts. My dad did it too. When the thoughts are debating, the tapping ignites—my dad would say."

"Yes, Dad too." She sighed and her smile softened. "Thanks for the reminder of my dad."

Her soft expression and expressive words touched him. He hadn't told her that right now the tapping was happening because she was so beautiful and he was sitting in a chair across from her. His fingers had been keeping rhythm with his heart, which was about to blast out of his chest despite him not wanting it to.

"Please," she said. "It's peaceful out here and you can thump your fingers all you want, it doesn't bother me at all. I actually like it."

She liked it. He smiled. "That's okay, I don't always need to thump them and I needed to relax a little bit as you can tell. I always drive through town most evenings. I have great deputies but after I've been home a few hours, checked my cattle and ate my supper, I come check the streets one more time. I did it with my dad years ago when I was in school. It was a great time. When I got into high school and athletics, I didn't have time to do it. But, now it's part of my job."

"That's a nice memory for you I'm sure. And I bet the town loves you for that extra care you give your job, along with everything else you do, like catching rustlers and helping them catch bad guys. Or helping stop fires that Doobie and Doonie start accidently at the town gatherings. Though I believe they're better now."

He laughed, liking this conversation. "You read Maggie's column. She tells fun things about the town before answering letters in her column."

"Yes, I am a reader. That's what brought me here. But I noticed that there's been no mentions of fires lately that Doobie and Doonie start while frying turkeys." She chuckled. "I knew I was moving here when I wrote the bid for the motel, whether Pebble sold to me or not. Maggie's column is wonderful and it drew me here."

"She is a great writer. And yes, Doobie and Doonie have gotten better, we've all gotten better. Now when we set up to cook turkeys or fry fish, like this weekend, we make sure the roasters aren't anywhere near the tents. We have a great *volunteer* fire department made up of local cowboys who would rather be herding cattle than putting out fires. They don't want things burning, but we have learned how to handle it."

"That's great." She leaned back in her chair and looked at him with a gentle—gentle was a good word for her.

But he'd seen little sparks in her eyes earlier that said she might not always be so laid back…he wondered about that. He yanked his thoughts off of Lara, he didn't need to wonder anything about the new motel owner.

"I guess Pebble prepared you that we love people coming to town and we have a lot who come to our events. Especially since Maggie's articles shined a light on our town. When the nice lady came to town things changed in a good way. I got to watch my three buddies, the Monahan brothers and their great granddad, he's their granddad but he's a great man, so the great granddad is who Pops is. They struggled so much after what their not-so-great dad had left behind after he had gotten addicted to gambling—and no one knew it."

"It was a bad thing…" She paused and looked up toward the moon that was showing, something had changed in her expression.

"Does that strike a chord?" Why was he asking that question?

She looked at him. "Yes. My dad and mom died in a plane crash too. Last year."

Shock filled him. "I'm sorry."

"Me too. But, my dad was a wonderful businessman and a great dad, and it was a sad loss. It has been a hard year, but Maggie's articles helped me and brought me here. I feel bad for the Monahan brothers, but they're strong and I'm happy they overcame what their dad did."

He couldn't take his eyes off of her. She was point blank, told him like it was. And drew him like dynamite. "They did. You seem to be doing good too."

"I'm moving forward. Maggie mentions you in her articles and tells readers they need to find someone in town they can talk to if they fear they are in trouble or need help. And in Wishing Springs, that's you."

"That's my job. I want to help anyone who needs it. I try to be on alert as…" He hesitated, trying to find the right word.

"You watch people?"

"I watch everyone. Newcomers when they come to town. I watch for stress, signs of trouble. I keep my eyes on them until I understand them better and feel they are safe. That's my job."

"So do I. You're here now watching me."

It wasn't a question from her but a statement. He'd set himself up for that one. He gave a small smile. "No. Believe me, I knew before you arrived that Pebble had done her checking. Her husband is a great reporter and owns the newspaper. He knows how to check people out. No, Pebble wouldn't have sold her place to anyone who was bad. But that being said, if you need anything I'm here. I'm sure you saw my number on the bulletin board in the office. If not..." He stopped talking while he reached into his shirt pocket behind his badge and pulled out a card. "Just in case it's not there, here's your own card."

So do I. Her words that he'd overlooked in the you're watching me statement echoed in his head as she took the card from his fingers. Her fingertips brushed his and instant awareness of the woman in front of him slammed through him.

Put him on alert.

CHAPTER FOUR

Lara took the sheriff's card, Jake's card, and their fingertips touched as she did so. Sparks shot through her and she snatched the card, almost crumbled it as her fingers clutched it tightly from the reaction.

What was that? "Thank you," she grunted, like she'd been sucker punched in the gut. The mere touch of this man got *that* reaction. She shoved it away, not going there.

Instead, forcing herself to speak in a clear, normal voice, her mind seeking something to say that sounded normal. "Pebble warned—I mean told me that you would be checking on me regularly. She said—well it doesn't matter what she said, thank you for stopping by." She stood. Time to get him back in his truck and on his way before she fumbled any more words. Old habits in stressful times were bursting through her.

He stood. "Is something wrong?"

"I'm going to have a big day tomorrow. I'll be baking cookies. I bake them and freeze them like Pebble did. I'm carrying on the tradition. Customers will be coming in next weekend so I must be ready." She was talking fast but had to get him gone. "And the ladies told me they supply refreshments for people so I thought I would bake some things to give away." Why was she rattling on, it was *pathetic*. "I also need to start making a list of things I might want to change or update here at the motel. Not that I'm changing much but Pebble told me to make it mine. I will, but very carefully thought out." *No careful thoughts right now!*

He stood barely two feet away with the table no longer between them. Her heart was racing faster than her words had been, thundering, rocking her stomach like she was in a boat on rough ocean waves.

His expression dug deep, looked concerned, then he stepped away, thank goodness. Relief washed over her, and as if seeing that he took another step away. She took a breath, only then realizing she'd barely been breathing.

"I'll be around," he said, his eyes digging. "If you need any kind of help, call that number and either me or one of my deputies will be here. And again, welcome to town." Then he turned and strode around the back of his truck and to the driver's side door and climbed in.

She stood frozen as he fired up the engine and then drove the truck in a large circle so he now faced the exit. He lifted his hand, that was now resting and tapping on the open window sill. And then he was out the drive and on the road heading the way he'd come.

She just stood there watching him, then sank into her chair. What was wrong with her? She was here and it all felt right except for her reaction to the handsome sheriff.

And that was not something she'd expected. And in *no way* wanted.

* * *

Jake didn't sleep much, he'd sat on his back porch late

into the night and now sat behind his desk at the office. Two days had passed since Lara had moved to town and he had had her on his mind a lot. She'd been at church yesterday morning but he'd stayed at the back like he normally did, keeping watch to make sure the service was safe. He was always on guard, even in the Lord's house.

Now, he finished his paper work, then pushed his chair back and stood, he had a meeting at the community center. Today had been his late day, his normal day to leave and drive around before he headed back to his ranch, so that didn't give him much time. He said good night to his deputy in the front room and then walked outside.

He didn't make his drive through town but instead headed home to get ready for the town meeting. He'd had the urge to drive by Lara's just to acknowledge her with a wave as he drove by. If she was sitting outside, letting her know he was here if she needed him, but he wouldn't stop. She just needed to know he was here and she was safe, that was his job—his job, nothing else.

He headed home, took a shower, and then dressed

in a black T-shirt rather than a starched sheriff shirt or a starched western shirt, tonight he was going casual. He added worn jeans he worked on the ranch in and his cowhide boots that had walked many pastures and ridden many horses. He headed out the door to show up at the town meeting about the upcoming Saturday event. He'd be on duty at the Wishing Springs Tossing Extravaganza. But tonight was a casual meeting and he could relax.

Lara might be there and he still had everything about her on his mind, the sensations he felt when their fingers had touched. A small, simple brush of her fingertips as she'd taken his card had felt like an explosion in his chest. And it had shaken him up, still had him shaken and it had been two days since that touch.

He hadn't gone to The Bull Barn for lunch, and stood watch at the back of the church, then left before everyone else left. Being at the back made that easy. Parking at the edge of the parking lot did the same, got him out of there before anyone else.

But this wasn't a big city, it was a small town where

everyone cared about each other, and got together like tonight. Distance from the new member of town would be hard. But it was clear she wasn't interested and he wasn't either. The undeniable fact that she had an instant effect on him that he'd never experienced before was just there. He didn't have to pick it up, didn't have to let it have an effect on him.

So, tonight he would begin the task of getting comfortable being around her—keeping his undeniable attraction to her under wraps.

He pulled into the parking lot of the gathering place and he was glad to see trucks he recognized. Business owners who would participate in the fun day serving and helping out at the booths, would see a lot people showing up to have fun.

The Monahans were here already so he headed their way. "Hey," he said. All three couples welcomed him. He got a handshake from Jarrod, one from Bo and one from Tru, then a hug from all their wives, Maggie, Abby, and Cassidy. He smiled as their names popped through his mind, all with the same ring to them. Lara's name slammed into his mind, a different sound to her name but she fit with these ladies.

Jarrod slapped the chair beside him. "Saved this one for you. Have a seat."

"Thanks. You know me, I always feel a little odd when I show up in my not official gear."

"Yeah," Jarrod said, looking serious. "That's why we added more deputies to assist you in your job to protect our people. You're past due to more time in regular clothes."

Tru and Maggie were sitting in the seats in front of all of them. They'd turned so they could look at him and their other family members. Tru looked serious. "We needed them, especially after having all that rustling going on. But you needed more time off."

"Plus," Jarrod said from beside him. "We hear there's a new lady in town."

Bo leaned forward from where he sat on the other side of Cassidy and his wife, Abby. "And she seems nice."

Abby smiled. "The ladies said she's *really* nice."

Cassidy, touching her hand to Jarrod's arm briefly, studied him. "I hope you'll go by and check on her like you always did for Pebble."

He glanced and saw they were all zeroed in on him. "I check on everyone. I went two nights ago and visited with her. Let her know me and my men are looking out for her business and everyone else."

"That's great, Sheriff Morgan doing his duty," Cassidy said, her eyes digging. "Maybe tonight you can talk to her as a citizen. You are off duty, right?"

Uncomfortable, he tried to hide it. Yes, he was an officer of the law, he investigated and solved problems. But it didn't take any of that to hear and see the excitement in Cassidy's eyes and voice and in all the Monahan's expressions.

He zeroed in on Jarrod. "Okay, what is going on? I'm not looking and you know it."

Jarrod held his gaze. "Maybe not, but you could. And if you haven't heard about it, there is a lot of talk going around about you and the new lady in town. There was a diner full of people on her first day in town and you had lunch with Tru. Must have been some tension or sparks flying since everyone in there noticed it."

Bo added, "No one said anything at church

yesterday because they were all still watching and everyone saw you had slinked out during the last prayer."

He stiffened. The whole town was watching him. "Yes, I did. I do that sometimes when I have other things I need to check on."

Maggie tapped his knee from her seat in front of him. "Relax, don't get all worked up. I'm not writing about it unless you write a letter to my mail link." She smiled.

"*Never* happening. I'll let everyone else write in for your advice."

"Lara's nice," Abby said. "We met her a few minutes ago, before she got surrounded. Everyone wants to meet her."

"She is," he agreed before he could stop himself. "But y'all know I don't have time for anything other than keeping this place safe. I'm sure y'all heard that one of my deputies went out to the Martin Ranch the other day where a cow was found dead. It's probably a coyote but it's not looking like it."

"We heard that, but we're just glad it's not rustlers.

If you think it wasn't a coyote, then what?" Jarrod wasn't smiling anymore. None of them were.

He leaned in for their ears only—like he hoped the entire conversation had been. "Actually, sounds like we might have a panther or mountain lion passing through. Something bigger than a bobcat."

The ladies gasped, glad he had large-cat-talk to get them off of the beautiful-lady-talk.

Tru frowned. "So, me and my brothers have been so busy we missed hearing this?"

"You're not missing anything. We're just checking it out. A mountain lion has a large radius they travel. Hopefully it's heading out of our county and no other cattle will be lost. My deputies are going to be checking around, asking questions of everyone, so we'll see if something else has happened that we haven't been notified about."

"We'll be checking this out too," Jarrod said. He ran the cattle part of the Four of Hearts Ranch while his brothers each had their specialty. Tru trained, showed, and competed with the champion horses while Bo built excellent stirrups that everyone waited to get on his timeline. The man was a worker but had a family now and hired more help, still, his business was booming as were his other brothers, so hunting a mountain lion probably wouldn't be on their to-do list.

He'd hired deputies to help take care of some of this stuff. And he'd decided to let them take this on for now. He had to give them some leg room; just had to watch and make sure they did a good job. Maybe he did need to slow down a little bit...maybe. His gaze shifted to Lara across the room. She was surrounded by ladies, including Clara Lyn and Reba, who were at the head of the crowd.

The woman drew him like fire on dry pasture land, yes, he was dried up no matter how much he wanted to deny it. He'd had his future all laid out, hadn't thought about a woman for a long time, and then she drove into town. Now she was all he could think about.

He took a breath. "I'm going to get a drink," he said, stood up and headed to the drink table. He didn't need to talk at the moment, especially to his friends who had been studying him. Hopefully they hadn't followed where he'd been looking before he got up.

Now, before the meeting started and everyone sat down he needed to get something to moisten his really dry throat. He had a woman on his mind, the undeniable attraction drew him like he'd never been drawn before. His gaze locked on Lara's blue eyes. They were lit up with happiness, and the smile on her face as she talked with the ladies added to the beauty of the moment.

His heart rammed him in the lungs, stealing his breath away. Yanking his gaze off of her he spun to the water jugs and prayed a long drink would clear the smoke in his head.

* * *

Lara focused on the ladies, smiled at their excited comments of how glad they were she was giving Pebble the freedom to enjoy love again. She was trying hard to ignore the most handsome cowboy in the room. She'd noticed him the moment he'd walked in the door and refocused on the lovely ladies surrounding her. He'd been sitting but now he was heading toward the drink table with determined steps.

She knew what was on the table because she'd already been there: sweet tea, unsweet tea, homemade lemonade, sodas, coffee, and water. Water is what he went for.

Trying not to watch but unable to stop, she'd caught him staring her way—she'd yanked her gaze off of him and focused on the sweet lady talking to her. Then before the next lady stepped up and took over, Lara's gaze shot back to see Jake fill the paper cup again, tip it up and practically suck it down. Shocked and unable to look away she watched as he did it again, then he abruptly crumbled the paper cup, tossed it into the trash can as he spun back toward her and caught her staring— She sucked in a breath, feeling as if she was standing on wet ground as lightning struck her, took her breath, and she was going to pass out—

"He's a handsome guy, isn't he?" Clara Lyn nudged her, laughing softly. "Caught you two ogling each other."

Yanking her gaze away from Jake she looked into the bright, twinkling eyes of the hairstylist. "He's great looking," she managed, then declared, "But I'm not interested."

"You've *got* to be, he's not just handsome, he's an amazing man," Reba declared in dismay as the group of ladies surrounding her nodded in agreement.

Lara *had* to get her brains back. "Ladies, I'm *not* looking for love—I'm here to enjoy life. Alone and *unattached*." To anyone with love, she said to herself. Friends yes, but never love. Her heart couldn't handle the loss again. "I'm here to continue carrying on my wonderful motel's reputation created by Pebble. It has an amazing reputation and I want to be a great host. I'm *not* here looking for love. Or a personal relationship." The song Looking For Love In All The Wrong Places played in her head. Been there, done that, and never again.

"But why?" one of the ladies asked.

"Look, my parents are rooting for me from heaven to have a new life. I was always a very quiet person and very protected. But, I've chosen to step out and live life my way and that's what they would have wanted. I'm living here because I want to make people feel at home, in my way. So, relax, ladies. And remember, I think Jake is just as determined as I am to stay single. On that he and I agree. And we are the two that count." There, that had been point blank.

Clara Lyn dropped her head to the side. "I'm so sorry your parents aren't with you here on earth, but I have a feeling they are echoing my thoughts from up above. Life isn't just about working—I love my work but I have a life too."

"She's right," Reba said. "You have to step out sometimes. Take a risk on love, and I think your parents are rooting for you too. We would all love to see our sheriff find love. We're not saying you and him are a match, but checking out the draw that we see between you means finding out where it leads. Maybe to love."

Did they not hear what she'd said? Of course, she hadn't said everything and she didn't plan on it. Some things were better left completely out of a new life. A jerk wanting her money, not her love was enough to make her use all the fighting skills her dad had put in her...and she did use a sucker punch—she almost laughed remembering that, then shoved it away, her gaze found Jake's once more. And sucker punching that masculine cowboy wouldn't have the same result as her other one had.

And actually, looking at him, it wasn't socking him in the gut that crossed her mind; it was kissing those firm lips that slammed into her and had her yanking her eyes from his. But the thought stayed whether she wanted it to or not.

CHAPTER FIVE

After locking gazes with Lara and knowing she had witnessed his thirst—yeah, thirst—what was he thirsting for? *Love*. No, this was crazy.

He set himself back into his chair, didn't even look at Jarrod, knowing the cowboy was watching and recognized tension when he saw it. Thank goodness Doobie and Doonie stepped onto the low stage and started the meeting. They were both on stage but just one was the acting mayor.

Doonie—yep, he knew which one was Doonie, he had a slightly higher hitch to his left eyebrow and he was the actual mayor. Once he'd figured that out, which was only seeable when the two were together, he'd kept it to himself. When they were separate it was hard to know, as in coming to the meetings as the mayor, there was only one at the meetings. Not that anyone let on whether they could tell them apart. So, standing up there together, he was pretty sure that sometimes Doobie acted like the mayor just to throw everyone off.

He was the sheriff, an investigator and that was his job to see the differences. Though it was hard to find, he'd seen it right after he'd met them. He figured if anyone else figured it out, they knew how to keep their mouths shut too.

Now the two men grinned. "Alright, here we go," Doonie said—the real Doonie. "We're going to have a great day next Saturday. Now, for those of you, like Lara, our new motel owner, it's going to be her first day to experience Wishing Springs having fun. You'll get to know us all and we *promise* we're not going to burn anything up, so you won't get to experience that fun."

"Thank the good Lord!" Clara Lyn called, and the entire room busted out laughing.

He didn't. He was just glad they'd gotten the original fire out last year and everyone made it. Thank goodness.

* * *

Doonie and Doobie were up on the stage. She had to get their names straight but right now, her mind was rumbled because of watching Jake. The sheriff had rattled her brain and she still didn't have it back. Now, one of the twins, while talking, looked straight at her.

"Is that okay with you, Lara?"

Startled, she yanked her crazy thoughts off where it had gone. How long had he been talking to her? She'd been distracted and hadn't heard a word. "Sure, that sounds great."

"Awesome we thought that would be a good thing for you to take part in."

What did I just agree too? "What do I need to do?" She threw it out there hoping she sounded normal.

Both brothers grinned. "Well," the *not the mayor* Burke brother said. "Since you're new in town and Pebble, being a smart woman, had closed the motel with the knowledge that you were coming to town and would possibly buy it from her. Whether you would or not,

Pebble and our buddy Rand went off on an adventure. So, the motel was going to be closed this week, so that gives you time to chip hunt."

Chip hunt. She glanced around the room, and everyone had turned to look at her, grins on all their faces. Her gaze shifted and caught Jake looking at her to. He didn't exactly look happy—what did he look—aggravated? Agitated?

"You don't have to," he said, as if giving her fair warning. "I can handle it on my own."

Oh goodness, he was saying he could handle—what? What had she missed? Her mind had gotten stuck on the handsome sheriff and she hadn't heard a word. But everyone was watching her. "No, no, no, I'm fine with it. I'll be able to do it."

Jake nodded then looked back at the brothers. "Alright, we'll get it done. No worries, I know how to find the right ones so we will find them."

Find what? Thankfully, the fellas took the attention from them and started directing everyone else on what they would be doing to get ready for the following week's gathering. And she absolutely had no idea what she was about to do. All she knew was she would be doing it with Sheriff Jake Morgan. How had that happened?

The next hour passed quickly with her sitting there uncomfortable, seeing grins from Clara Lyn and Reba and wondering what she'd agreed to. But, defiantly, she was determined not to ask. Whatever it was she was sure she would find out. Jake, she'd tossed glances his way, was sitting one row back giving her a great view of him. He had said those words and now looked straight ahead.

He hadn't looked to the left or the right but then she hadn't kept her eyes glued on him because no one needed to see her doing that. No one needed to see how flabbergasted or lost she felt. But she felt it. Finally, the meeting was over and though she had no idea what she's agreed to, she slipped out the door and headed to her car. Needed to be driving down the road with the top down and the wind blowing in her face. Waking up is what she needed.

Calming down is what her heart and head needed.

Breathing hard she made it to her car, fumbled the keys, dropped them to the ground, of all things. She bent down to grab them but a long-fingered, strong hand beat her to them. Jake's hand. He picked them up and held them between his thumb and forefinger for her to take. She held her ground and looked at him. He wasn't smiling, though his eyes couldn't be seen beneath his hat and the darkness of the night despite the parking lot light being a few feet away.

"Here you go," he said.

"Thanks." She opened her hand, palm up, taking no chance of touching him again. He dropped the keys in her palm but they locked gazes as her fingers closed around them too quickly, and—*drats*—brushed his fingers as she did so. "So, what are we doing?" she managed, ignoring the raging fire that shot through her.

His lip hitched to the right side and his head tilted, now his eyes twinkled as the parking lot light touched them. "I wondered if you somehow missed what you were agreeing to. I wasn't sure how, maybe you were talking to the ladies when you agreed to gather cow patties with me."

"Cow *patties*?" What was he talking about? Surely not what she thought that meant.

"It's a well-loved event and we need a lot of cow patties. So, you agreed to help me gather them over the next few days. We'll be looking for dried cow patties. Cow chips."

"Oh my goodness," she gasped, then realized she'd said it out loud. Loudly. "I'm going to look for cow—" She halted her words. He was nodding. His eyes twinkled with loud humor. And her head did a somersault and splatted against her ribs, like fireworks sending her entire insides into an explosion.

She couldn't speak. Heart pounding, she just stared at him.

"You did miss what you agreed to do. Do you do that often, agree to things you have no idea what you've been asked to do? It's not really a good or smart thing to do. I have to tell people all the time not to get in the car with a stranger if you're stuck on the side of the road. Just get in your car, lock the doors and barely roll the window down, and tell anyone who stopped to help that you've already called the cops. In your case, you spoke and agreed to something before understanding what you agreed to. Before I had the chance to warn you about acting too quickly."

She sighed, as he hitched a brow.

It made sense and was something her parents had warned her of being a single gal. It's not a good thing to do, agreeing to anything before you know what it is. Or like her dad always said, *"Never except a drink of any kind from anyone that you didn't pick up from the counter yourself. And never walk off and leave it sitting there for some sleaze bag to drop something in, something that could hurt you or cause you to pass out."* Her parents had prepared her for everything because they worried about her from an early age. Overprotective, some would say, but they didn't understand why her parents felt that way—they didn't know the depth of her father's success, and he never wanted her to be used because of his wealth.

But this wasn't to that degree, thank goodness, but still, *what* had she agreed to? Her dad's protective words of concern hung in the air. *"If you break down on the side of the road, call me, and I'll be there."* He loved fast cars because he could use one to get to her or her mom as fast as possible. If he couldn't get there, he'd call for backup closer to her. But he was no longer here. No longer around to worry about her. He was just above, rooting for her to find her own way.

She breathed deeply. She had been overprotected even as old as she was. Their protection had put fear inside of her and now she'd overcome that fear, she was a middle aged woman, not a child. She was responsible for herself now. No one else. And that was the way it would remain.

Her father's love for cars had been for him to never lose her again. A memory she was too young to have but a memory that stood out in her father's mind, so he'd become overprotective, even when she was in her thirties. Even when he'd realized he might have been part of her problem. The life of a rich girl wasn't as easy and perfect as many people believed.

And she was proof of it.

Still, she loved her parents with all of her heart, and she'd kept the car they loved to ride in together. And this had been his favorite, it was fast in a split second and could stop on a dime. Two of the most important features of a car. Right now, it could get her away from the cowboy if she was inside, but no, she was standing beside it. Like her father had planned for her to do, she'd auctioned off the amazing collection of his cars for top dollar. All but this one.

Now, here she stood with a great escape vehicle and she couldn't move.

* * *

Jake was speechless now as they stared at each other. He told himself to take his eyes off of her but it wasn't happening. Especially since she hadn't taken her eyes off of him. They had a connection. The rumbling and the tingling inside his chest told him it was true. He only had that reaction when he looked at her or he knew he was on to something and he had to get it out or someone got hurt. Like the night he had to race out to Jarrod's to try and save him and Cassidy from the cattle rustlers.

Speak. "Yeah, I normally do it alone every year on my ranch. The ladies knew that, and I think they thought you going out on some ranch property would help you get adjusted to living in our town. And in the country.

We have beautiful country around here. And I personally like my place. I have a good number of cows so, there is a lot to pick from running up and down my hills, and since its summer and not raining, it's a good time to fine, dried cow manure—to be frank." He hitched a grin. "It will be easy finding them,. We have a lot of people coming to town these days, and I don't understand why, but people like to throw cow chips. But more than that, those that bring their heavy-duty turd shooters like to shoot them too."

She gasped. "What did you say?"

He laughed. Couldn't help it. He had known he would get a reaction but not one quite so blunt, alarmed. "Well, there are some who come, and right there where we hold it just outside of town there is an open field. There are lots of other towns and states that do it too. People have created an amazing mechanical *chip* shooter. They are machines, and they're all makes and models that shoot them through the air for a long way. So, there is hand tossing and machine tossing. The winners in either one whose fly the longest yards wins." He stopped talking and grinned, he couldn't help it, the woman look flabbergasted. He gave her a moment.

"Okay, so this teaches me from now on to never say yes to anything that I don't actually hear what I was saying yes to. I'm not going Easter egg hunting, I'm going—well I can't actually say what I'm going to do—it just doesn't sound right coming out."

"You're going to be looking for chips. Cattle chips, how does that sound?"

A hint of a smile came to her shocked face. "Okay," she managed. "Chips. We're going to gather chips. Not potato chips or Barbeque chips but chips."

He couldn't help it, he started laughing. And he put his hand on his stomach and tried to tell himself to shut up. He couldn't help it then as he laughed even harder her eyes opened wider, and then she grinned, and then to his startled surprise, she laughed too. And oh goodness, the woman laughing was wonderful.

Her smile was huge and her eyes crinkled too. But it was amazing and he was so floored that his laughing subsided as hers did too. "So, glad you're laughing now, not passing out or getting upset. Welcome to Wishing Springs. Pebble used to love to throw the chips. Little tiny lady that she is couldn't throw them far but she loved it. And her first husband, he was excellent at it. It was as if he was throwing a discus, and he often won. But after he passed away, everyone tried to do better. We have a variety so if you're interested in trying it—"

"*No*, I'm not."

"You can wear gloves while we gather them. I can come and pick you up in town if you need me to."

"I'll drive. Just give me your address."

"I do have a good driveway up to the house so your car will be okay, if you'd rather drive."

"I'll drive," she said again, no ifs or maybes involved.

He still hadn't gotten over the fact that she had moved to town, bought Pebble's motel, and she drove a Porsche 911. A red sports car, not a brand new one but fairly new and that meant it was loved, or inherited it or just bought it when the price was right or she liked to go fast—quickly.

He liked driving a truck, he was a rancher and for his job the SUV could go fast, helping when he had to catch a runaway. But a Porsche 911 he knew could fly.

So her car could fly. He laid his fingertips on the hood. He had to ask, "This is a beautiful car. Am I going to have to pull you over? Are you a put the pedal to the metal kind of lady?" He hitched a brow.

She chuckled and it rattled his insides. "Well, I have to say I have, at times, a need for speed. But my car can go from zero to sixty miles an hour in less than thirty seconds or less. When I was younger, I got to ride with my dad and he was a great driver, a man who concentrated on everything around him when he did it— I'm not saying it's right. But when he took me for a fast ride, above the speed limit, we were on a race track and he was teaching me when and why there is a need for speed. He loved it. Me, it's about the jump in speed when I need it and also feeling the wind around me when I need it. Besides, the speed limit has caught up to the speed I love, Sheriff." She smiled and his insides somersaulted. "But I don't break the law, unless there's a moment of need. Safety is always on my mind. You won't be having to pull me over."

"A fast car gives you safety." It wasn't a question, he felt her assurance in her voice when she said the words.

"Exactly."

"I'm glad you feel safe. My job is to help keep people safe in a sports car or even a regular car and those around them. It's my job to make sure people aren't negligent behind the wheel."

Her expression hardened. "I can assure you I'm not negligent. When I'm behind the wheel, my hands are in the ten o'clock and the two o'clock positions, yes, I know it's changed now to the nine and three o'clock positions but either way it gives me the control needed while my gaze is watching ahead of me. Watching for an escape route in case there is a wreck or oncoming disaster or—I'm a very focused driver and any avenue I'm walking down. So, no worries I won't be the one you have to come after."

His mind was spinning at her fast, precise words. This woman had an unusual way of wording things. Her intense gaze told him nothing about what she just said in a lighthearted, humorous way. It was all very serious. And he believed her.

It seemed this woman knew her way out of bad situations. Why?

Watching for an escape route in case there is a wreck or oncoming disaster or—her unfinished sentence filled his thoughts. She cut it off and then said she was very focused.

What did she not say? *Or*—

What came after or?

"My dad and my mother loved riding in this car. And overall that is why I kept it. My mom didn't have the need for speed just the need to be with my dad." She smiled. "Me, like my dad, I have the need for speed, but I kept this car because it was their most loved car out of his collection. They'd just bought this one before their plane crashed. They'd had it for a month."

"I'm so sorry. But I'm glad it helps you with your loss." His mother had left everything of his dad's behind when she'd left after he'd died. He had the ranch and his dad's old four-wheeler…he hadn't ridden it in a long time. Maybe he needed to take the cover off and check on it.

"I'll keep it forever as a memory I share with them." Her words brought him back from his own family casualty. "*But,* I realize now, me driving this car and owning a motel are not going to go together. There's not enough room inside of it to carry anything. Especially anything for the many rooms of the motel. Plus, I only want to drive this car when—" She stopped talking and looked away. "Sometimes I just need a drive. So, I have a single-car garage behind my motel apartment. I'll keep my 911 stored there out of sight and I'll get a larger vehicle for my daily use. Probably an SUV that I can carry things I might need for the motel in. So, yes, I'll have a more appropriate vehicle sitting outside my motel and to drive down country and rocky roads."

He hitched a grin. "Sounds like a plan. Just remember you're in the country now, and on country roads you have to watch out for more than just cows, deer, and hogs. Those are among the largest to watch out for but squirrels, armadillos, skunks, and possums need to be watched out for too. Swerving to miss any of them can lead to a bad accident. An SUV would be good for safety reasons."

Jake was just doing his job with the warning, no other reason...not the overwhelming need for her to be safe or the want to pull her close and see if her heart was pounding like his.

"Thanks for letting me know and I'll head to the motel now. I don't know where you live though?"

He pulled a card from his pocket then a pen, and put his address on the back. "Just plug that address in on your phone and it will bring you to my ranch. I'll be up anytime, so come when you want—"

"I'll be there about eight. My dad always said an early start makes a good day. He started earlier." She smiled.

"I do too, but I have some things to do before you arrive so eight is great. I'll see you then. I'll have most of the day, because I don't go in until the evening tomorrow."

"You work a lot."

"Yes, I do. That's what I was born to do, so no worries."

She nodded then reached for the car door but he beat her to it, their fingers meeting at the car lever. He had to start avoiding those fingers of hers as heat raced through him. She pulled her hand back and he opened the door. She quickly slipped into the seat. He carefully closed the door and watched as the car roared to life. Then she pushed the button that sent the top folding away behind the seat. He stepped back as the engine hummed like it had been waiting for her to join it in an adventure.

The thought of him joining in on the adventure slid through Jake as Lara turned her head and looked at him. She gave a quick wave of her fingers before placing them on the steering wheel at the two o'clock and ten o'clock positions, steady and ready for anything. Then she drove slowly forward from the car's backed in position.

Jake stood still, watching as she carefully drove to the entrance, turned onto the road and drove away…leaving him with the lingering revved-up need of starting a new adventure in life that included Lara Strong.

On that need he slammed the door, he wasn't going there.

CHAPTER SIX

S he was *really* going to his house to go looking for cow manure—*chips*. Lara almost laughed, she'd get that word right sooner or later. They certainly weren't about to gather potato chips today!

Cow chips.

She concentrated on the country road with that *"cow chips"* ringing through her head like a song. Just as it had done since she left him standing in the parking lot watching her leave last night. She had been set up and tried to tell herself not to be upset about it. She should be, but she couldn't get past the idea that she was about to spend the day gathering chips with Sheriff Jake Morgan.

Cow chip hunting was the craziest thing she'd ever

imagined. And yet the conniving sweet town, the trickster twins and a certain couple of ladies, Reba and Clara Lyn, who were obviously a hoot to be around, were all rooting for this set up that had happened last night.

The one thing she had to admit was Jake, there in the crowded room, had asked her, as if clarifying, if she wanted to do this? He hadn't known when he asked that she had no idea what she had agreed to. But still, he had asked the important question. And she'd said yes or whatever she'd said, her brain was cloudy at that moment.

She focused now on the very long country road that he lived down. His ranch was off the paved road. This was a beautiful red dirt road that had huge trees meeting each other overhead, making a stunning arch tunnel. It was picturesque and the morning sunlight made speckled golden spots on the road like a speckled road of gold.

Almost like God was making her thoughts sparkle with encouragement. She could do this.

She.

Could.

Do.

This.

She was a little mixed up right now but doing okay. She was pushing herself to be more out-there rather than held-back, which was normal for her.

She'd just reached the end of the trees and into the full bright sunlight surrounded by green pastures spreading before her on both sides of the red dirt road. Her phone's map told her Jake's ranch entrance was the next right. And a black iron fence led the way. It was totally stunning seeing the rolling hillside and the black cattle roaming through the grass and horses grazing with them. It was beautiful.

Up ahead she could see the black iron fence was leading to a tall entrance gate—suddenly a deer leapt over the fence on the left side of the road, it practically flew through the air and landed right in front of her car—she instinctively stomped the brake hard. Slammed her foot to the foot pedal bringing the car to an instant, firm halt as the deer sprang toward the black iron fence. Startled, Lara watched as the beautiful deer landed like a ballerina—thank the good Lord—a few feet into the pasture. Then it raced across the pasture, through the cattle that thought nothing of the deer racing through them.

Lara couldn't move, just sat there stunned watching the show as the graceful, *alive* deer disappeared into the thick mass of trees in the distance. She could have hit that beauty.

Thank goodness her brakes had worked and her reaction, a well-trained reaction she'd learned from her dad and his many lessons on escaping anything and everything, had worked in that instant. Thankfully, she'd never had to test her reactions often in real life.

Breathing hard, she was so thankful her father had worked with her on her reaction. He'd always preached that before he bought a vehicle he tested it. He drove it, looking for two things: that when he pressed the gas it instantly jumped forward like it was a racehorse at the starting gate, if the car hesitated at all it was a no-buy. Second: stomping the brake, when he stomped, it stopped. He always preached that a hesitation when you needed either the brake or the gas was a no-buy. When you needed to get out of the way of an oncoming vehicle or stop before getting hit, it was a life or death reaction. And his teachings had just saved that deer.

It could have been a kid or a family.

She totally got his reasoning. This car did it all and she'd just tested it out and it passed with flying colors. Thank goodness.

She closed her eyes, said a thank you to her dad and the good Lord before pressing the gas gently and turning into the ranch's driveway. She crossed the cattle guard beneath the iron entrance that said across the top in large letters *Morgan Ranch*. She followed the long white rock road that led to a large stone house with a metal roof and a chimney. It was Texas all the way and further back to the side was a large red barn and stables. And Jake stood tall and masculine at the entrance of the barn. Hands on his hips, his cowboy hat scooted back on his head, clearly showing the alarmed look on his face. He now strode her way with long, determined steps.

She parked, her heart still pounding—yes, from the deer, but it was also now racing because of the sheriff. He was the sheriff and that was the reminder not to let this crazy attraction that she could no longer deny rage through her. Yes. She'd admitted it.

She was attracted to the cowboy.

The man with an expression, a manner—everything that drew her.

"Are you alright? That was a hard stop you did to avoid hitting that deer. I should have warned you before you drove out to be on the lookout for them."

"I'm fine."

He stopped in front of her. "They cross the roads regularly, especially there where they have the protection of those trees and then the protection of my land and trees. They don't normally, well, if you had been warned to drive cautiously, then you wouldn't have had to experience what you just did. I'm sorry."

She raked her hand through her hair and hitched a grin, a bit of a fake grin but it was there because she was determined not to look upset *or* attracted. "Thanks. I have good reflexes, and the car has great brakes, all due to the preaching and training of my dad."

"Smart man looking out for you."

"Yes. Now I know I'll definitely be buying a big

SUV. Like you said, something not so low to the ground, and that I can carry supplies for my motel. That beautiful deer helped me on that decision, and also, like my dad taught me, the brakes and gas need to work instantly and powerfully like my car's just did, protecting me and that beautiful deer."

* * *

He liked that. "You had a very smart dad. My vehicles do that, so even if I wasn't a sheriff, I'd be judging a car or truck by its reactions, not its attraction, its beauty."

"Exactly." She smiled and he reminded himself that he wasn't looking for attraction to her either but it was here.

He'd looked forward to her joining him on this job today more than he had looked forward to anything in a very, very long time. Maybe ever.

That thought struck him hard. "Well, I've got the truck loaded as you can see. All those buckets are ready to be filled. Do you need anything, coffee, water, bathroom? Anything, breakfast—" He grinned.

"No." She laughed. "I'm good, it wasn't too far of a drive, of course I may need a bathroom break later, or is outside behind a bush my only choice?"

He chuckled. "We can head back to the house anytime needed. We have to eat too."

"Sounds good. This will be an all-day affair?"

All day sounded good to him. "Yes. We have a lot to pick up." He walked to his truck and opened the passenger's door. She'd followed him and now moved past him to the truck. Instantly her faint pleasant scent drew him like she did and he was tempted to lean in closer.

Focus.

He stepped back and let her get into the seat on her own, though he wanted to offer his hand to her. She slid into the seat in a quick flash, needing no help. He closed the door then strode quickly around the front of the truck, climbed inside, and focused on their mission of the day. Not on the sense of connection radiating through him as he looked at her and she looked his way. He grinned, cranked the engine and decided to take it.

This was going to be a great day. Maybe the best

day he'd ever had hunting chips.

* * *

"Your ranch is beautiful," Lara said, taking in the beauty as they drove down a road that headed toward the deeper sections of the ranch, and trying not to feel the draw she had to the man in the truck with her. His wrist was propped on the steering wheel and he looked relaxed. No need worrying about having to ram on his brakes at this speed. He had the total look of a relaxed cattleman driving casually on the back roads of his ranch. It fit him.

"Thanks. It's been in my family for a long time. My ancestors came onto this property in a covered wagon, and it's been in the family ever since."

"Seriously?" That was cool.

"*Seriously*," he copied her tone and shot her a grin that made her laugh. "Many ranches in Texas started that way. They worked hard, and then my grandparents worked hard, then my dad followed in their steps, and my mother loved the ranch too. When I came along I worked it, as my dad had become the sheriff here in town and split his time between both. But being sheriff came first for him. The ranch and family history was important to him, but keeping Wishing Springs, including me and my mother, safe was number one for him. As it is for me now."

She focused on the property and not him as they drove through an open fence, over another cattle guard into a pasture stretching before them. There were no cattle or horses grazing here. A peaceful wave of beauty lay before her and she was drawn to it. It was like a painting with trees off to the left and to the right, the great open land that had a small lake in the center. It was perfect.

"So, this is the chips and dip pasture?"

He laughed. "Yes. The cows love grazing, eating the oats and making the chips that people love to toss after the sun does its job drying them out."

"It sounds like it's all worked out." She couldn't help it as the words came out.

"You are funny, Miss Lara Strong."

"My dad said that too." It was true, sometimes

things came out funny, but Jake had set this up, and she'd followed his lead. Just like her sweet dad often did, and they laughed a lot.

"Now the strong sun has done its job. All of their business is dried up and ready to be harvested," he said, adding to the humor and making her grin widen. "So, it's chip harvesting time and I usually do it on my own. But today I have a partner. Are you *sure* you want to do this?"

She chuckled again. "I just can't believe this is something *normal*, but yes, I'm just going to let you tell me what to do and lead the way. You've done it all this time so you're a professional chip picker-upper and about to teach me."

His grin matched hers. "I've never thought about it like that, but I'd love to teach you to become a professional chip picker-upper. You could help out across state lines, maybe make a living picking chips up for other county chip tosses."

"Are you telling me that people do this in other places?" He'd halted the truck and now focused his astounding brown eyes on her.

"Yes, it's been going on a long time. In history when people found out they could toss a chip, competition started. If you look it up, it goes way back, even in the Olympics for a short time but was quickly removed, or tossed out."

"No way," she gasped unable to believe that could be true.

"Read the article. I read it a long time ago, before so much junk was in the computer world like now that you have to question if it was real or fake. Fake is a big thing these days. Anyway, I think it's right."

She was going to look it up and probably chuckle the whole time. Cow chip throwing all through history, what a hoot.

"Now we get out and go to work." He opened the door. "Meet me at the back of the truck and I'll show you how it's done. And seriously," he said, looking back over his shoulder before he exited the truck. "If you don't want to do this, you don't have to. And that's all I'm going to say, you can pick to or choose not to, and it's all good by me. We're out here now so you can just watch me pick them up if you want to."

"I'm going to try this." She sighed, but determined. Then she got out of the truck and met him at the back as he let down the tailgate and handed her a new pair of gloves. "Wear these," he said, then pulled two large buckets to the edge of the truck.

She slipped on her thick rubber gloves like she was going to go to work cleaning the floors in the kitchen, not pick up cow chips. But that was exactly what she did over the next four hours.

They walked around that large pasture. It wasn't just picking up the chips, she had to have a little shovel to slip under the hard, dried up pieces of—poop. Then she laid it in the bucket, then went on to the next one. And one thing was for sure, she might come out here and pick them up because she had said yes before knowing what she'd agreed to, but there was no way she was going to join in the competition by throwing a chip.

But...there were a lot of buts, she had to admit it would be interesting watching other people tossing them. Thankfully, after she'd learned how to pick them up, Jake went one way and she went the other. Giving her some relief from...his nearness. Now, stand here making sure she didn't put her gloved hands on her hips, she had her palms out so the back of her gloved hands rested on her hips. It was a little awkward but gave her a moment to rest her back from all the bending as she took in the view. Jake was in the view and as if feeling her gaze, he looked her way and smiled.

And her pulse increased despite her not wanting it to.

"I think we've gotten all we can get here," he called. "Come on and head back to the truck." He picked up his tenth or maybe twentieth bucket and she picked up her seventh or ninth bucket, she'd lost track. The one good thing was that the dried up chips didn't weigh a lot, but they took up space. When they got back to the truck, he pulled his gloves off and laid them in the corner of the truck bed.

She did the same, then took the wet wipes he offered her from the plastic container. Her hands had been safely concealed in the gloves but this was more welcomed protection. "Thanks." She wiped her hands and he wiped his too, then he placed his wipes in a bucket and she did the same. "Glad that's done. It was an experience to say the least."

"Yes, it was. Are you ready to eat something and take a break?"

She hadn't let her thoughts go to lunch or a break for the last four hours but now, well, it was time for a break. She squinted at him in the sunlight, trying not to like the smile hitching up the corners of his lips and or the lift around those amazing sable brown eyes. "Yes, I have to admit I need a break—a bathroom break." She gave a comical grimace, hopefully that was what it was, grimace.

"Me too." He closed the tailgate and walked to her side of the truck, opened the passenger door. "Hop in and we'll head that way."

She stepped between him and the truck's seat, her gaze latched onto his eyes like a magnet. Her feet paused instantly of their own choice.

"I'm glad you're going to stick around," he said, putting his palm on her elbow and guiding her to step up into the truck cab.

Thank goodness she did as he directed. Her heart was doing erratic flips as he closed the door and strode around the truck toward his side, as she fought to halt the chaos going on inside of her. He'd simply touched her elbow.

But even that wasn't what had stumbled her, it was simply looking at him and suddenly wondering why no woman had ever won his heart. And what it would feel like to kiss him. Or for him to kiss her?

And that was what froze her to the spot until he'd touched her, gently urging her to get in the truck.

And now, her heart was off to the races, but she wasn't sure what finish line it was trying to make it to. She looked out the passenger window and not at him as he climbed inside the cab.

She had to get a grip and get it quick.

CHAPTER SEVEN

After the trip to his house, a nice house with a lot of wood, leather couches, and wooden floors that were manly, but then on the walls were some beautiful paintings of the land . She only saw the large kitchen and the living room as he led her to the front bathroom and he headed into the back part of the house. When they finished their bathroom trips, they unloaded the filled buckets then loaded more empty buckets and headed out again. She'd spent a moment in front of the mirror, telling herself to stop looking to see if she looked alright. How she looked didn't matter.

Now, they were heading over a large incline and when the truck topped the hill, Lara broke the silence with a gasp. "Beautiful." And it was.

Down the hill was a large lake, not huge but this was definitely a lake. The one that morning was definitely a pond. Trees lined the far side of the lake and a blue sky highlighted it. "The picture in your living room."

"Yes, my mother painted it," Jake agreed. "Like this lake, the painting has been here a very long time. We'll go down there and have lunch on the pier. If we're lucky, the bald eagle, like the one you saw in the painting, may fly over. He has a nest nearby."

Lara loved it. "You've got a little bit of everything here."

He hitched his shoulder. "Not everything, but it's a great place."

"It is. And an eagle to top it off."

He drove down the hill toward the pier. "Do you eat here on the pier often?"

"No. I haven't actually sat down on that pier since, well, I was probably twelve when me and my dad ate down there while fishing. As the painting shows."

She heard the tone in his voice. "That's you and your dad in the painting. What a talented mother you have. And what a good memory. One day you can fish here with your kids."

"I won't have kids. I'm not planning on getting married. It's a bit tough when I think of it. Shouldn't have mentioned it."

He wasn't ever getting married. "Why?" The question came out before she knew it was coming. "It's none of my business. Sorry."

Why wouldn't this well-respected, strong, protective cowboy, she could just see that he was probably an amazingly loving cowboy, get married? Great husband material. *And why are you, Lara Strong, having these never-ending thoughts about him?*

Looking straight ahead he pressed the gas pedal and they eased down the drive toward the lake. "I don't ever want to leave a family behind."

His words touched her. She had been left behind, and she didn't plan on getting married either. She couldn't stand the thought of losing again. But she'd not go there, but living a life alone didn't seem right for him.

She knew love failed, had faced it and didn't want to face that again—she pushed the thoughts away. "My dad and mom never planned on leaving me behind that soon. It's been a very rough year, but I'm moving forward. I cherish every moment I had with them. They're forever in my heart."

He pulled to a halt at the lake. "I was a senior in high school during football season, at the first of the school year when the call came. I was on the football field when it happened."

Her heart clenched. "I'm so sorry," her voice trembled. She could see him as a football player, probably an amazing player given his size and defined muscles, even now. But none of that mattered when your heart was breaking in grief.

"I'm sorry for you too, and so recent."

She looked at him and he at her and an emotion seemed to flow between them. An emotion that had nothing to do with the attraction she felt for him, whether she wanted to or not. "I'm so sorry you were only in high school. I had mine longer."

They continued to stare at each other and she felt closer to him because they had this awful connection of losing their parents. Thankfully he still had his mother.

"Your parents sound great from what you've told me. Mine are too—my dad *was*. Your dad knew how to help people make money, make a living. My dad helped them live a safe life."

"Now you follow in his footsteps." Tears swelled inside of her but she fought them off. She never cried anymore. She'd cried so hard in the first few months but her dad kept telling her in her heart to get over it and move on. It had been in her thoughts, she knew he wasn't standing there in front of her but it always felt that way. "Where's your mother?" she asked, needing to move the talk of death out and talk of life in.

"She lives in Florida now, in a retirement community that's safe. She's fifty-five, a great parent but didn't handle my dad's death as well as my dad would have hoped. I have to take her into consideration on every move I make. I'm all she has. Thank God, that she truly understands I'm driven by my desire to be an officer of the law. Your dad was driven and taught you how to succeed. In your mindset, not mattering if you did what he did or did it in your own way. Me, I followed in my father's footsteps, despite my mother pleading with me not to do so. But like you hear your dad in your brain, I hear my dad telling me to move forward and go on and I have. But…" He paused, his eyes turning to the water.

Hers did too. She saw a cowboy and a young cowboy sitting on the pier, a fishing pole in one hand and a sandwich in the other. Her heart clenched. It was a beautiful visual.

"I," he started again. "I see me and my father out here on this pier, but I won't ever see me and my child out there. I have my mom to look out for, and I haven't been able to open my heart, no matter how much I want to, how much I hear my dad telling me to. I can't risk leaving someone behind with the pain my dad left my mom with."

Unable to stop herself, she reached her hand out and placed it on the forearm connected to the hand that was still gripping the steering wheel. "You do what you have to do. You chose to live life the way you need to do it. That's what I'm doing. I understand what you're doing. I get it. And I'm sure your dad gets it too, looking down from heaven."

There she'd said it. She prayed her mom and dad got it looking down on her. She had no desire to feel that loss again. Her love for her parents was strong. Oh, so strong. But an attachment to a spouse, to her husband would be even greater. And to a child…that she couldn't do. Didn't want to think about. Yes, she was a chicken. But she'd also found out right after their death that the attraction she'd had toward the man in her life then had been a lie. He'd only been after money, and that had been the sledgehammer to her heart. Yes, she was a chicken in more ways than one.

And she was okay with that. Her heart had nothing hanging onto it and that was how it would always be. Pain was never going to have a hold on her again.

* * *

Lara's hand felt gentle on his arm and Jake felt it all the way through him. That soft caress, filled with care and understanding. Her words were soothing and not condemning, telling him he needed to look for love like he felt in all the eyes of the people in town. Thankfully they didn't push him, they just loved him and enjoyed the service he did for them. And that was enough.

Unable to stop himself he pulled free his hand from the steering wheel and gently placed his palm over hers. "Thanks for understanding and I just have to say I think the town is really happy you're here. And you're going to fit in like you were made for Wishing Springs."

"I'm so happy. That's what I felt every time I read Maggie's articles. They drew me. And I finally listened. Even though we lived in a great place in the city, I felt trapped because of what I wasn't going to do with my dad's investments. Even though I've spoken more about my dad, my mother was always there for me. And she, I can hear her saying, go for it. Make your own steps forward, not ours. Follow your dreams and so here I am."

She pulled her hand away and he felt a loss as he instantly reached for the door but had to say, "I'm glad you listened to her soft voice. She sounds very gentle and caring. Like my mom, she didn't and still doesn't push me to do what she wants. She just lives her life and prays for me. And I try to make sure she has security knowing that I'm still here."

"I would have liked to have met your dad. And one day, if your mom comes to visit, maybe I could meet her. Just—" A shocked look took over her face as she paused her words. "Just because you have said such wonderful words about her."

"Well, it's nothing against you but she won't be coming back here. I can tell you that when I tell her that you're in town and who you are and how you act she will say she's glad you're here. And—" What was he about to say? "She would be praying that I don't find you attractive or enhancing enough to want to marry. Because she doesn't want me to die in the first place and certainly not leave anyone like Dad left her."

"No worries," she said instantly. "I get it because I'm not looking. So, let's just say, let's leave all that behind and go out on that pier and have a good lunch. I've actually enjoyed this day, this talk. Unbelievable, yes, but true."

He laughed, feeling a relief inside. "I think we are in total agreement. I have thoroughly enjoyed chip hunting with you. Now, let's go eat."

CHAPTER EIGHT

Jake made it through the day with the new beauty who was in town. Lara had startled him with her story. She had heartbreak and was afraid of, basically, the same thing his mother was afraid of. If she married, she would go through an even deeper hurt.

His mother still lived her pain and he didn't want to make it worse, but now he got to see her pain through the beautiful Lara's eyes and heart. It had stayed with him all week. Now, he stood in the pasture staring down at another dead cow. And instead of thinking about what had killed the cow, he was thinking about what had hurt Lara.

He shook his brain and instead of thinking about yesterday he concentrated on the look of the dead cow laying before him. It was as if it had been put through an operation of its chest area. Some would say an alien had done this, and some would say other bad things had come, but he looked at it and knew that it was a mountain lion, cougar—a wild cat was roaming his county.

"Sir, do you think it's a mountain lion?"

The deputy's words reached him, told him he hadn't been concentrating. "I'm pretty certain. Good eyes, Deputy. Now, this tells us that he's still here. They have a large radius, and he is still in our county. They don't normally eat a lot of cows, usually other smaller animals, but this one seems to like cattle. We need to alert everyone to be aware and not to go on long secluded walks and not at dusk."

"Yes, sir, we'll get the word out. I'd hate to think it would take down a person." Deputy Kevin said.

"I'm with you on that. You get that started, and I'll get there in a bit after I talk with these cowboys."

"Got it." Looking serious, Deputy Colten walked away after tipping his hat to the three men standing there silently waiting.

Jake focused on the Monahan brothers now.

"You agree with us?" Tru asked first.

"Yep. No doubt about it. I'm sorry it's on your property."

Bo pushed his straw Stetson back on his forehead, exposing his grim expression. "At least we're aware of it and caught it in time to alert everyone. My Abby and toddlers won't be off the porch."

Jarrod put a hand on his brother's shoulder. "Ease up. It won't come up to the porch or the barns where we have all our horses—"

"I can't say that's the truth," Jake said. "It came to the second pasture of the Ross's front porch. They found the cow dead right there over the fence. I'm pretty sure it's moving cross-country, so it may be out of the county soon. But we still need to be on the watch."

And they would. He just needed to get his head on straight and take care of business. He and Lara had gone out again once more and gathered chips but they'd stayed away from personal topics, she seemed as determined as he was not to go there again.

But that hadn't taken his mind off of her and that

was bothering him. He had a job to do.

* * *

Lara had enjoyed her first week in Wishing Springs. The town was wonderful. She'd picked the cow patties with the sheriff two days in a row, and now, thank goodness for distraction from an attraction she didn't want. She'd gone shopping for the motel—which she was tempted to change the name to the Sweet Dreams Inn. It sounded a little more up to date and she liked the sound of it. But she just wasn't sure. She loved it being the Sweet Dreams Motel and needed to give it some thought— keep her brain busy.

She needed to make sure before she ordered a new sign—another brain-busy motion. Thank goodness she could put all that on her mind and distract her from the cowboy who kept interrupting her thoughts. Thoughts she didn't want interrupted. She was here to open this motel, and so she'd busied herself with going shopping and replacing a few things in each room with her touch. Bedding, pillows, a few pictures on the wall.

Something, anything to keep her mind where it needed to be. She'd stuffed the small trunk and the passenger seat and foot area until it was bulging and knew and SUV was in her future.

And today it was time to go to The Cut Up And Roll hair salon. She was parked right in front of the salon and got out of her low-riding car and walked to the front door. Before she could open it the door flew open and there stood a smiling Clara Lyn.

"Welcome to The Cut Up and Roll. We stayed out of your way while you were getting moved in. We promised Pebble we wouldn't overrun you while you were settling in. But here you are, so come on in."

"Thanks for the welcome. I have been busy with the motel and the chip hunting."

Reba grinned. "Did you love collecting cow chips with our handsome sheriff?" She was working on the fingernails of a grinning lady with curly dark hair.

"Let's just say it was an experience. And thank you all so much for the set up. I think I could have been mad, but didn't go there. Funny, ladies."

The room instantly burst into laughter.

Clara Lyn patted her on the shoulder, her bracelets singing as she pointed at a styling chair. "Have a seat darlin'. We promise we aren't matchmakers, we just couldn't help ourselves. Jake is handsome and nice. And a great cowboy and we know he would make a great husband—"

"I took it as a setup, but ladies," she said calmly, looking at all the beaming faces. "I'm not looking for love in all the right places or wrong places. I'm here to run my wonderful new motel."

Reba stopped working on the beaming lady's fingernails. "And did you have fun with our sheriff?"

The rounded lady getting her nails done picked up a thick paper fingernail file and slapped Reba's wrist. "Stop, you know we're not supposed to be meddling into other people's lives."

"Bertha, you hush. I just wanted to know."

Bertha grinned. "If you haven't figured it out, I'm Bertha, the nurse in town. If you ever need me, just come to my office down the street. I'm there three days a week and they will tell you if I'm not there to go see Doc Hallaway, the vet here in town. Yes, he can fix dogs, cats, cows, and anything else. And yes, if you have a cut on your finger, he can help. But I'm just letting you know not to judge me by this conversation right now. If you need me, please trust me and come see me. But I'm praying you don't need me. Health is a good thing and I like it. Now, Reba, you going to finish my nails or just sit there and intimidate this new lady in town? The lady y'all set up to pick chips with our handsome cowboy sheriff. Me, I don't want to pick up chips but I do like to watch people chunk them and some people can really chunk them far."

Lara stared at the bodacious lady full of quirk. "I'm really glad to meet you, Bertha, and I'm hoping I don't have to come see you either. But thanks for telling me where your office is and I really hope I don't have to go see the vet. Unless I get a dog or a cat but I now own a motel and don't need one there. But thanks for the info so I'll know where to go if I happen to need it. Now, all of you, come on, not everyone is looking for love—"

"This is the right place," Reba sang. "You know the song Looking For Love In All The Right Places, this is it." And then she turned and started working on Bertha's fingernails as she hummed the tune, and then she got slapped with the file again.

Lara looked at Clara Lyn. "What?"

Clara Lyn winked at her. "Yes, I winked. But we are going to try to leave you and our cowboy sheriff alone. He is an amazing man and we just wanted you to know that."

"He's a strong, loving man," Reba added, looking over her shoulder. "He loves his mama with all his heart. He lost his dad, it was sad and his mama hasn't gotten over it as far as we know. She left soon after it happened. Having a husband who was the sheriff and was killed while helping a family on the side of the road changing a tire—it was horrible, sad. And she didn't want her son to follow in his footsteps but he did."

"His mom is really sweet," Clara Lyn added. "We love her and pray for her. She blames him being a sheriff on his death but he was a great cowboy and would have stopped and helped that lady and her children whether he was a sheriff or not. Still, she's blamed his job and worries about Jake."

Lara's heart clenched in that moment. She hurt for

the poor woman—the woman she did not want to be. This conversation fortified her determination to never be in that position. "Just so all of you know that I'm happy. Really. I came here to watch love happen and to hang out with you gals who are so wonderful. But if y'all only give me a hard time talking about Sheriff Jake or finding love, then I'll just hang out at my motel. And go to another town to get supplies and my hair cut. To be honest, I'm not here for that. I'm just here because I like y'all—at least I liked y'all from the mentions in Maggie's articles. I'm just looking for a place to call home among friends."

All three of them stared at her with wide eyes and distressed looks.

Reba laid her nail file down, scooted her rolling stool out and jumped to her feet, her fist on her hips. "Honey Darlin', don't go getting upset. No, no, no. We are good. We want you here. We don't want to run you off. If we run you off we'll be in trouble."

Bertha hooted. "Oh yeah, they'll be in trouble alright. Pebble is a sweet angel but she'll be mad. Pebble is the one who always knows when people come to town things will happen with or without our help. Or their help, I just watch from the sidelines and see the show."

Clara Lyn stepped over and put her jingling bracelet-clad hand on Lara's shoulder. "Honey, we promise you that we'll try hard to stay out of your way. We want you here. We want you to have a good life. So, let's go back to having a good day and stop messing things up. What can we help you with? You've got your motel ready for guests and your cookies made? Tomorrow your guests will start checking in, right?"

Relief flooded over Lara. "Yes, tomorrow the first customers will be checking in, that Pebble knew what to do. She booked me up, gave me the week to get ready. Told me to settle in and I did. I bought a few things to put my mark on the place. It gave me something to do and now my handprint and hers is on it. *And* I made the cookies because I love that gesture. I love to bake too." She was so relieved that they wanted her here as much as she wanted to be here.

"I'm going to tell you," Clara Lyn declared, waving her jangling hand in the air. "Our Pebble has a new life. She loves that sweet Rand with all of her heart. And they are living it up, so I can guarantee you that motel was a wonderful benefit to her. It helped her live her life, gave her something to do when she grieved her first husband. And then kept her busy while she was trying to deny that she loved Rand. She had to watch him fight drinking himself to death because he couldn't deal with never having her love him."

"Thank the good Lord they are on the right road now," Reba added. "And moving forward."

Bertha gave her a firm look. "Sweet Pebble isn't going to be upset about anything you change or do to your motel. It's your sweet dreaming place now to find happiness or comfort in."

Clara Lyn grinned. "Whatever it takes for you to make that motel yours, do it and she will be cheering you on. And so will we."

Goodness, this was exactly what she'd dreamed it to be. She blinked back tears, feeling her parents smiling. Their silent, shy child was still alive and well. And she could feel their happiness surrounding her.

This wonderful town was now her home.

CHAPTER NINE

Lara was loving *The Chip Toss Extravaganza*. Obviously the night of the meeting, everyone hadn't mentioned the name of the gathering or she might have gotten the hint. She laughed thinking about that night. She wasn't upset at all, she loved these people, shenanigans and all.

She'd brought cookies, *containers* full of them. Around six or seven dozen, she'd stopped counting and just filled the covered plastic containers full. When she'd walked to Main Street with her arms full of the boxes, she'd taken them to the booth that belonged to *Over The Rainbow*. It was a wonderful place for unwed mothers who couldn't keep their newborns but wanted someone who would love to adopt them. She met Peg, a midwife who had opened the wonderful home and her daughter Lana—a counselor.

"Thanks for the cookies," Lana said, then grinned. "You know the moment I heard Lara Strong was the new owner of the Sweet Dreams Motel, I couldn't wait to meet you. Now that we're both residents, I'm sure our names will get a little mixed up."

"Probably so. But I'm thrilled to be mixed up with a woman who does such wonderful things for these young ladies. And their babies."

Lana looked touched. "I love my job, my life."

"All I hear are great things about what you and your mother do helping everyone. If anyone is going to make money off my cookies, I wanted it to be y'all."

"Thank you. We always appreciate donations in any form. Especially delightful cookies."

Lara said nothing but had come prepared with more than the cookie donation. She'd learned that all the entrance money for the chip tossing contest would go to help support the wonderful place. She liked how the town showed their goodness and God's goodness through the home for unwed mothers. Any young woman torn about having an abortion or saving her baby and letting a family who needed or wanted a child to take care of her child was a hero in Lara's heart. So she gave her cookies, and after Lana had headed off to help someone, Lara glanced about, and seeing no eyes on her, she slipped an envelope into the five-gallon plastic container for donations. It was well guarded by Peg, Lana's mother, the founder of the home. But Peg had turned to check on someone and in so it was the perfect moment to give.

Then as Lara strolled around the gathering with nothing left to do other than say hi to people, monitor her phone in case a reservation request got forwarded to her—yes, she'd updated that part of her business. Now, she wouldn't always be stuck behind the desk. After all, the place was booked and they were all here so she'd come too. It was all good.

Then, she spotted the sheriff. Her pulse increased and she told herself to *get a grip*. Jake was down the street surveying, watching over the crowd. Standing guard, she was sure. He had safety front and center of his mind and she saw his deputies scattered throughout the crowd. They were also very watchful, taking care of business and smiling when needed. But they, clearly, were all making sure the streets were safe.

They were *watchful*.

She knew watchful, had been taught to be so by her dad from a very early age.

Lara turned and walked away stopping to watch the people as she went down memory lane… Her father had made sure from as long as she could remember, that she could take care of herself. But not everyone had had her dad. Not everyone had reasons he did for ensuring that if she ever needed to, she could take care of herself…or go down fighting.

She pushed that thought away, but knew it was true.

She went nowhere without having her eyes opened, watching, listening for anything, anyone who looked out of place. She knew at all times which way to go if something went wrong, always knowing a way out. Her gaze shifted around in that moment. It was crazy to some, but not in this day and time. And not to her parents. As a four-year-old she'd been taken, abducted, but not for long. Her dad had seen it happen and before she was stuffed inside a car he'd come to her rescue.

It had been a wake-up call for her dad. Her dad, who helped people make money because he was so good at it. But, he realized in that moment that she might be a target and he'd begun his overprotective security. After that she and her mother were protected. She was home-schooled and spent a lot of time at their huge home behind protective fences of stone and metal.

That day had changed their lives and had never been the same. Even now she watched for escape routes like her dad had taught her. He'd ask her questions like it was a game while he'd been testing her watchful eyes.

At first, knowing all these things didn't seem odd to her, because her dad had taught it as if it was natural. But as she got older she realized that she was always on the defense and also it kept her to herself. Later, she realized that her dad feared that someone might want to take her again, ask for money or harm her and their luck would run out.

He feared it so he'd taught her to take action. She hadn't known for a long time that the things he'd taught her weren't what most kids learned.

But as she was older, fourteen as a matter of fact, when she'd achieved her black belt and could also shoot a pistol, a rifle, and even throw a knife as if she were a professional. Yes, her dad had taught her to take care of herself. She could grab a man's thumb and take him down to his knees.

And her car—his car, any car she ever drove she knew exactly how to get out of any kind of trouble. She'd loved to ride with her dad, as he taught her how to press the gas pedal, shift the gear just right and swing the car around in a slide, then press the gas again and fly the way she'd just been coming from. Defensive driving had a different meaning when her dad had taught her on their many trips to the private race track that was also their private landing strip.

She'd learned that pressing the gas in the middle of a turn was a skill, and he could handle it better than anyone—and had spent time teaching her to do the same. She was a female version of her dad and had grown to love speed but only if needed. Her dad had taught her well and taught her to respect the speed limits. And that was where the top down helped satisfy that drive he'd built into her.

She just liked the pleasant feel of the wind. The freedom it gave her. It calmed her down. And like he'd always said, he prayed she never had to use what he'd taught her. He wanted her to have a normal life. So, here she was, living in this small town full of wonderful people, and she didn't think she would ever have to worry about needing to use those skills like her dad always feared she'd have to do at some point.

Yes, he'd prepared her but had hoped and prayed that she would have a calm life. He'd told her that he'd prepared her but hoped she never had to use it. And in the end, he and her mother hadn't had to use their skills. When their plane went down it had been in a flash because of bad weather and a lightning explosion. When their time was up they were both gone.

Now, standing on that sidewalk, her heart racing as she'd gone down memory lane, which always got her blood pressure racing, she calmed herself. She smiled, watching all the people having a good time.

She knew her father and her mother were smiling along with her. She'd found her way here to Wishing

Springs. It was now officially her home.

"So, you're having a great day?"

Lara spun around at the sound of Sheriff Jake Morgan's soft words. Thankfully she'd known his voice and hadn't reacted like she was capable of doing. Their gazes locked, moments before he'd been at the opposite end of the street and now he was standing behind her. His shoulder leaning against a post that held up him and the roof over the sidewalk. But looking at him, she felt like it was caving down on top of her. Her heart was on a rampage instantly.

"Yes, I am." She crossed her arms, needing something to hold her emotions inside. A disconnection between her and him with official arm crossing. "I was just looking about and calling this home. I love it here."

"That's good because I can tell you that everyone who has met you is really glad you're here. They know that this was where you were meant to be."

"I think so too. I'm at least glad to be here. Everyone is having a great time too."

"We have a lot of gatherings. You missed the spring gathering with all of its homegrown strawberries.

Cassidy Monahan, she's married to Jarrod and has her granny's homeplace, which is a Bed & Breakfast. She raises strawberries, peaches, and all kinds of fruits and vegetables on her place. Plus, a host of animals. She's done a lot there this last year. She has her booth right down there." He nodded to the left. "I could introduce you to the whole Monahan herd right now if you want to meet them. You walked out of the meeting the other night before they got to be introduced."

"I did walk out." She chuckled, thinking about it. "I'd love to meet them. And see Cassidy's booth. I need to stock my refrigerator."

"Then walk this way, ma'am." He waved his hand out to start the walk.

They walked beside each other and she tried to ignore the flutter of her heart when her shoulder brushed his arm, but it was there no matter how hard she tried to shut it down.

"You and your deputies have really made this gathering into a safe place. That's a good feeling."

"I need you to know if you ever need me, you've got my number. Right in that phone of yours?"

"Yes, I do." She'd put his number into her quick calls, not because he drew her but because he was the sheriff, and if she needed anyone, she was ready to call. She'd told herself that was the only reason she'd put him in the number one spot. That was where her dad used to be, but he no longer needed a phone. But he was looking down and she knew he was happy that she had put Sheriff Jake Morgan's number in her phone.

* * *

Jake was relieved as they approached Charity Monahan's table, packed with all kinds of fruit she raised on her property. Tru, Bo, and Jarrod stood talking off to the side and watching over their toddlers and their grandfather who was standing there with his hands on his lean, jean-clad hips, watching his grandkids playing. But the instant he spotted Jake coming their way, Pops made a quick path toward him the moment he spotted them. "Jake, thought you forgot that today we're heading to a cutting competition."

"No, Pops, I didn't forget. Are you ready to ride?"

Pops had Alzheimer's but was a number one cutting horse champion in his long career, and still competed in his mind.

"I am. Who's your mate?"

Jake almost choked at the startled gaze Lara shot him. "This is Lara Strong. The new owner of the Sweet Dreams Motel. Lara, this is Pops, the famous and wonderful horse trainer and rider."

Lara's confused look cleared as she smiled broadly. "*Pops*, it is so nice to meet you. Your career is outstanding."

The little man's eyes twinkled. "Nice to meet you too. You're with a good man right here. I always knew that he'd find the right woman one day. Good to know you're finally here. We're about to get busy with the show and then the fireworks start. That'll be great. Yep, sparks are about to fly." He winked, then strode back toward his grandchildren.

All the Monahan ladies were standing at the table smiling at them, obviously hearing Pops' words.

"Lara, this is the Monahan family," he said, very aware of the looks on their faces, like they'd liked Pops calling Lara his mate. They were smiling and so were their husbands as they stepped closer but still had their kids in their view. Great dads they were, and loving every moment of their new lives as husbands and dads. He tried not to focus on how that was suddenly starting to hammer in the back of his brain.

"I'm Maggie and I'm so glad to meet you," Maggie held her hand out to Lara, who took it instantly.

Jake saw the happy look in her expression—meeting the woman whose articles she'd said she read obviously made her happy. He liked the look on her face.

"I'm so glad to meet you," Lara said. "All of you."

Maggie shook her hand after placing her free hand on top of Lara's in a very welcoming gesture. "These are my sisters-in-law, Cassidy and Abby. We're glad you've moved to town."

"Yes, we are." Cassidy took Lara's hand as Maggie released it. "When Pebble told us she was selling the motel, we were shocked. But, we knew that she would pick someone special to take her place."

"So true." Abby, her eyes sparkling as she held her

hand out for a handshake of welcome.

Lara smiled, as she took Abby's hand. "Thank you all, I couldn't resist after reading all of Maggie's wonderful articles and watching the interview on television. I was drawn to this town already, and when I saw the motel was for sale, I didn't hesitate."

Abby's smile softened. "It's a wonderful motel in a sweet town. When I came to Wishing Springs, I stayed at the Sweet Dreams Motel. It was a haven for me, *after* I hit a bull in the road and met Bo." She smiled at the handsome cowboy who was smiling at his wife.

Lara seemed touched by the couple as they looked at each other. He couldn't look away.

"I'm so happy for you. I feel like I know all of you a little since Maggie mentions y'all in her opening statements before she focuses on helping people who've written in to her. And she mentions the town and your family sometimes as examples."

Maggie smiled. "Yes, everyone is good about letting me make mentions of their happily-ever-afters. And then Pebble and Rand got married and they let me mention them too."

Cassidy added, "We are so glad those two admitted their love at last. Are you here looking for love or are you like me and *not* looking? My Mr. Right over there changed my mind and I'm so happy about that. But you have a serious look in those blue eyes of yours."

Of course, that question had to come up, and Jake saw Lara looked hesitant standing there. He would have hesitated too—now, since this lady had come to town. Before she'd arrived there wouldn't have been no hesitation at all.

Lara found her voice, "I'm here to start a new chapter of my life. But looking for love is not part of that plan. I'm looking forward to running the motel—and becoming a part of your wonderful community."

Jake let her words sink in. He needed to get his thoughts back in line. She wasn't looking and he wasn't either, so there.

Suck it up, Sheriff. Get your game back in play: not looking for love was where he needed to focus. That and the protection of his town.

CHAPTER TEN

"How was cow chip hunting," Maggie asked. All three Monahan ladies were smiling as Lara finished saying she wasn't looking for love. Cow chips helped her and she laughed, couldn't help it. She felt at home with these ladies.

"Fun actually. I got conned into that, as y'all saw at the meeting, because I was distracted and didn't hear that I was agreeing to "hunting cow chips" but Jake was good." She glanced his way and he looked…strained, stressed. Unable to stop herself, she smiled at him. "Jake helped me learn how to hunt and find great chips. We actually had fun searching for the huge amount of them. They're now stored up safely so everyone can pick theirs today and then watch them soar through the air and sunshine today." He nodded at her, but his mouth was tight in a grim line and not a smile.

What was wrong?

Everyone was laughing at her words, and she yanked her gaze off of Jake as Pops ambled over.

"I used to fire them chips real good. I could throw them over a hundred feet. It was fun. Might do it today. Some people throw them wearing gloves. But they fly better if you chunk them barehanded." He held his wrinkled hand out with his fingers spread wide. Then he looked at her. "My hands...have been..." His expression turned dismayed or disappeared as if a cloud had come over him.

Lara's heart hurt seeing the fog in his eyes and expression.

Jarrod stepped up beside him. "Your hands are masterpieces, Pops. Your hands have given us a ranch and a life we'll never forget. Those hands know how to throw chips, but more than that they know how to gently tame a wild horse, ride the back of a horse like the fantastic trainer you are with them. Those same hands know how to hold our babies while you whisper sweet stories to them even when you're a little confused like now." He placed his wide hand in Pops and squeezed it gently as Pops took the touch and squeezed hard as he looked into Jarrod's eyes. Lara saw his wrinkled knuckles whiten with the strength as he held on.

Jarrod lifted their hands up a little higher, closer to his heart. "It is amazing what these two hands of yours can do, Pops. And all these grandbabies we are giving you will always know how much you love them and all of us."

Tears came to her eyes and she glanced at the teared-up ladies also watching. Oh, if her parents had lived this long she could imagine what she and her dad would be talking about. He had taught her so much. *So much*. Just like Pops had taught his grandsons that loved him dearly.

Her dad had been so protective and loving of her and her mother. He'd shown them all of his heart while he did the thing he was great at, using his amazing mind to help others. She'd been quiet as a child and he'd always tried to get her more vocal, more of a fighter and a protector. And with reason. She couldn't even think about her fate if her dad hadn't come to her rescue on that day when she was four.

She was fighting now to step out like her dad had urged her to be in his gentle and protective way. And it had taken losing him and her mom to make her take a step outside her comfort zone.

But she was trying to carry on her parents' legacy but from behind the scenes. She wanted nothing from it but the feeling that her parents were smiling.

She loved how Jarrod and his brothers were able to honor their granddad's legacy of goodness while he was still living. Even though he wasn't always with them. She prayed they cherished every moment God was giving them. And as she scanned her gaze about the group, she saw that they were.

"And all these grandbabies we are giving you will always know how much you love them and all of us." Those words rang out from all the rest. Her parents always wanted her to marry and have children for them to love. But she never would give them that. They were no longer here and she feared… Her gaze stopped short on Jake. He was studying her.

She was more startled to see his expression soften when he realized she was seeing him. He tilted his head in acknowledgment and instantly she felt a connection to the man. A connection she wasn't sure what to do about.

Or didn't want to think about.

Pulse racing, she tore her gaze from his and found Abby looking at her with her vivid green eyes that complemented her red hair. Abby stood out in any room Lara figured, and in that moment she needed the bright lady as a distraction.

As if understanding, Abby smiled. "You came to this wonderful town just looking for an escape? Right?"

Yes—she almost screamed but managed to just nod.

Abby continued. "I had a loss that I couldn't live with, and Maggie's articles drew me here. And God had a plan. I almost hit a bull before I made it into town and that handsome Monahan man standing there looking at me with those deep blue eyes I love, he rescued me from more than my painful past. He and my sweet babies were the plan. God's plan to heal my heartache was the right plan. So, what brought you here to buy Pebble's

Sweet Dreams Motel?"

"And start a life celebrating life here in our wonderful town and community?" Cassidy added.

Lara took a deep breath; all eyes were on her, and she was the one who had started this conversation. "I've had a wonderful life, but I lost my parents in a plane crash, like you," she looked at the Monahan brothers. "And I needed a new start. I read your column, Maggie. It gave me hope. I just felt like this was the place to start over and when I saw Sweet Dreams Motel for sale in your article, I wrote the note telling Pebble why I wanted to be the one she sold it to. But I was going to move here whether Pebble picked me or not. It just felt like the place for me to start over. But," she lifted a hand as if swearing on a bible, "I'm not here to be matched up. I'm just here to start a new life for me. I'm going to love helping people feel at home when they come to the motel. Like Pebble, I love baking cookies. I did it with my mom and it's a wonderful memory."

"Perfect," Maggie said. "Are you hiring more help?"

"I'll hire part-time help. And I have access to

everyone Pebble used to keep the motel going. And really, already I'm enjoying it. And I have all of you that I'm hoping to get to know better. It's only been a week and I'm really glad to be here."

With that everyone joined in on the conversation and she got a few more hugs from the ladies welcoming her.

Pops gave her a light hug that touched her heart. "Home is where the heart is," he said, his confused mind now seemed fully there. Then, he walked over to a fold-up chair and sat down to watch his grandkids playing. One of them, a dark curly-headed toddler, walked over and handed Pops a rubber horse he'd been playing with.

"Ride Pops," he said, beaming. "Me too."

Pops placed a wrinkled hand on the boy's shoulder and smiled as he took the horse. "Yes, you will. I'll teach you, Levi."

Abby placed her hand on her heart. "Oh, how glad I am to be here. That sweet toddler locked me into this wonderful world the moment I saw him as a baby."

The words struck Lara like an electric shock. What would that feel like? She didn't look at Jake but out of the corner of her eye, she saw Jarrod elbow Jake in the ribs. Jake gave a quick shake of his head and Jarrod hitched a brow. They were friends and Jarrod or all the Monahan brothers, knew that Jake wasn't looking for a long-term relationship. She got the feeling they probably knew why.

She hoped no one pressured him into trying to come after her heart when she nor him were interested in going that way.

Liar, liar, pants on fire—she shut her thoughts down instantly. And ignored what she wanted to deny.

Was determined to deny.

* * *

"Okay everybody, it's time to head over to the chip throwing," Jake called out to everyone, hitched a thumb in the direction of the end of the street.

Relief washed over Lara, she was ready to not meet his gaze every few minutes and have her insides going crazy. Thankfully everyone gathered their kids and headed that way. She went with them, grateful that the man redirected the focus from her to chip throwing.

Everyone began joking about the upcoming chip tossing as they walked down the street. Her thoughts needed to be on something other than the cowboy, the sheriff, the protective man that she wanted to stop thinking about. The man who had seen something in her eyes that had alerted him that she had things going on in her brain that she didn't want to think about and needed a distraction from. And he'd given it to her. Now he was leading the way toward the open field at the end of the street.

She was walking beside Abby and her and Bo's toddler, Levi. The kid was adorable. He was older than the other babies and very rambunctious. He was letting his mom carry him right now. Grinning widely at her.

"Chunk a chip," he declared, waving his chubby arm in the air. "I'm gonna chunk it hard."

His grit in his declaration made her chuckle. "I bet you chunk it far," she said, loving the way the little guy's blue eyes were beaming.

He clapped his hands and placed a palm on his mother's cheek. "Chip throwin' champ. Me, right?"

"Darlin', you and your dad have been practicing the chip throwing for toddlers. And you're going to be the champion, I think. If not, you're going to give it all you've got in that big muscle arm and enjoy yourself. Chunkin' it as hard as you can, giving it your all."

"Yep, right, Mama. Pops gonna chunk a chip too."

"*Yep,* I am," Pops said from behind them. He caught up and poked a finger in his grandson's tummy, making Levi laugh. "I'm gonna chunk it far. I've got that song in my head—already lost it. Chunk It, Chunk It...naw, Chip, Chip, naw, wrong. But we're gonna chunk it, you and me, little fella. We're gonna chunk it and chunk it hard."

Everyone surrounding her busted out laughing at the words as they reached the area where the town full of people were now gathered. They were lined up along two sides of the pasture and at the end of it where there were wooden posts with little blue flags. Boundary lines was what it looked like.

And of course, Doobie and Doonie Burke stood on a platform with a microphone between them. Doonie, the official mayor, she assumed it was him in his star-spangled shirt, was grinning happily as he welcomed everyone to the annual *Chip Toss Extravaganza* where they were going to have fun chunkin' the chips.

"As I said, all age categories. We've got male competition, female competition, and all different kids competition. We know some of you gals are toughies and can beat some of us men, but we can't take the heat, so you are in your group and we men are in our groups. Now let's get to having fun."

"Hang on, brother," Doobie said, elbowing his brother as he looked straight at Lara. "We want to give a very special thank you to our newest resident, Lara Strong, who helped our sheriff gather all these amazing chips. You two did great! Lara, you are going to compete, right? I heard a rumor that you weren't going to compete, say that's not true. You collected all these chips so you need to chunk one. I see those muscles in your arms. You look like you work out."

Everyone was looking at her. "Well, I do work out, but *no*, I'm not going to compete."

"No! You're going to compete," Clara Lyn declared stepping out of the crowd, putting her jingling

140

braceleted hands on her hips. "Girl, you picked them up, and surely you want to throw them. Believe me, you can do it."

"Come on, honey." Reba joined her friend, standing there looking at Lara. "You can do this. It's fun."

"I never planned to chunk chips," she gushed, exasperated.

"Look, honey," Reba continued. "These are chunky chips and chunk a long way. It's fun and a challenge to see how far you can chunk it. Come on and join the fun. I challenge you to see if you can beat me. I'm good. Real good." She ended her comments with the declaration that had a giggle racing inside Lara.

The lady was fun and had tossed out a challenge. Before Lara could say no again Reba stuffed her hand on her hip and gave Lara a look that drew laughter from the crowd.

"Honey, I can throw chips. It's not my favorite thing to do but I've got muscles in my arms too. I don't have them like yours and that's why I'd like to see how far you can chunk it because you must lift weights all the time. You have to be one strong woman."

She was a strong woman. She'd learned that, like

everything, from her dad. She was a heavy-duty weight lifter for strength and protection. A body of protection was what he called it. Her weight machine would arrive soon and she'd get back on her muscle building. Her strength training. And why, oh, why did all of this have to happen? "Okay, I guess I helped pick them so I can chunk them. But I'm not promising anything. To be honest, I picked them up with rubber gloves on." A lot of people laughed hard and her gaze landed on Jake, of all people, he had a half grin on his face.

"You can wear gloves to chunk them to if you want," he said. "And if you don't want to you can wash your hands afterwards. Some people who do it well, not sure I've witnessed anyone here doing it, but in the championships in Beaver, Oklahoma, they lick their fingers before they grasp their chip, and in between throws, because it gives them traction."

She remembered him telling her that and now, everyone busted out laughing. She laughed too. "Alright here we go." She couldn't help but smile big. Oh, the town she'd moved to. "Okay, I'm going to chunk it, and I'm going to chunk it hard. But I can promise you one thing: I am not going to lick my fingers."

CHAPTER ELEVEN

Jake had never had so much fun as he'd had today at the festival. The chip chunkin' had been the highlight, fun and hilarious. He and his men stood watch but he was glad he had his men because the truth was he'd been distracted.

As each person competed, his gaze kept going to the new lady in town. Lara threw her chip after Reba chunked her chip. Reba, the chunky little lady who loved chunkin' a chip, stood there with her favorite chip, and like a discus thrower, she dipped down, bent her knees, and spun like she was going to toss a discus and let it fly. It sailed into the air, wobbled and dropped like a heavy block of ice right there about ten feet in front of her. Everyone busted out laughing.

Reba put her hands on her hips and hooted. "I never was a very good discus thrower way back when but I sure enjoyed it. And I have good technique; a cow chip just doesn't have the weight and altitude gain as a discus. So, now it's your turn, Lara, and if you want a little advice, don't chunk it like a discus. Chunk it like a baseball that's the ones that win. I just enjoy it the other way."

Clara Lyn called out, "She's right, you've been watching all the others chunkin', so pretend you're an outfielder and chunk it hard and high, from the outfield to home plate."

A clear look of determination overtook Lara's sweet face in that moment. She stepped up to the line with her carefully chosen chip. A smart pick because it was about the width of her hand. She held it like it was a discus in her hand but pulled her arm back like she was an outfielder. Her dad had known what he was doing, he'd taught her to compete, realizing there was a chance in her life she might have to compete for her safe life. And he'd taught her well.

In this moment this was the woman who took after

the dad she'd talked about. She'd been quiet and looking for a quiet, calm life. But now her expression said she was ready to compete and he was totally entranced.

She stepped up, held her hand over her shoulder then, took three fast steps and chunked the chip high into the sky. It flew like it had wings, and it told him that somewhere between yesterday and today she'd watched and studied videos of champion chip thrower's technique. Chunking it hard and high like a baseball came natural to her, there was no mistaking that. The woman had an arm on her that knew what to do.

That cow chip flew and he had a feeling she was about to be the women's champion of all time. But in that instant, he knew he had a problem, a big problem; this woman had his attention in more ways than he wanted.

And right at that moment he wanted to take a step forward and hug her.

He wanted to kiss her, but more than anything, he wanted to sit her on his shoulder and let everyone celebrate the winning chip she'd just thrown.

She was amazing and he was in trouble.

* * *

It had been a great first two weeks in Wishing Springs. After the fun *Chip Toss Extravaganza* event she'd stayed and watched the fireworks with the ladies. The firefighters had put on the show and she made sure she stayed with the Monahan ladies and their children. And out of the way of the sheriff and his deputies, who walked around making sure everything was secure and safe.

She enjoyed her time with the ladies and she and Abby Monahan connected. She'd asked Lara to go to lunch one day and today was that day. And she was excited. It was Monday, the beginning of the third week since she'd arrived in town. Monday was usually a quiet day, she'd learned, in the small town. In a city, it was a busy day as business people checked who was in town for meetings. Small towns were different.

It was the weekends that were busier. Monday mornings were when everyone who hadn't checked out on Sunday checked out and left the motel quiet. One of the young pregnant ladies from Over The Rainbow, the home for pregnant ladies, showed up to clean Sunday morning and again today. Pebble had informed Lara about Vivian, the house cleaner, and that she was a pregnant nineteen-year-old, about to take a new step in her life. She was deciding if she would keep her child or let a couple adopt her baby. She'd come to Over The Rainbow on her own, without the pressure of anyone who knew her, and was trying to make the right choice for her and her baby. Working while thinking helped free her mind up as she geared up to make the right choice and Lara respected that.

She loved Vivian's attitude of determination to get her life in order and make the right decision. Lara respected that and was glad Pebble had hired her. Vivian had the week off since Pebble had closed the motel for her trip and in case she sold it to Lara.

Now, Lara's first weekend had come and gone, and Abby had called and invited her to lunch.

Lara hadn't hesitated, she'd instantly said yes. Abby knew a great place to eat and when Lara asked her if she might want to go look at SUV's with her, Abby said yes. She knew several dealerships in the larger city two hours down the road. So, they were making a day of it.

As soon as Abby drove up in her large, nice SUV that was built for a growing family, Lara hopped into the passenger's seat and off they headed toward the Woodlands.

"This is going to be a great day," Abby said as they headed through the backcountry.

"I think so. I'm looking forward to getting a SUV similar to this. My 911 is going to be locked in the garage. I'll always keep it and love it, but I'll drive it less. I need a larger vehicle to get me around and help out with my business. When I bought some things the week I was closed, I practically had to pile the passenger's seat ten feet tall."

"Yes, this is great for a growing family or hauling things. Your car means a lot to you, doesn't it."

"Yes. It was one of my dad's obsessions. He loved cars—a lot of cars. But he loved other things too, me and my mom included and at the top of the list." She smiled thinking of him. "But that car was his favorite and will always be with me like he and my mom are with me in my heart."

"I understand that." She patted the steering wheel with her fingertips, glanced at Lara, then back at the road. "I was married before I came to town and me and my first husband had an argument. I lost him and my unborn baby in a wreck during that argument. I didn't even know I was carrying a sweet child. It was so hard, but we were in a small car, though I love them, I'll never have another one Arguments are never good, especially in a car, but it can cause you not to pay attention. And that was the problem. Yours looks like it can go a high speed and out do most anything."

"Yes, you're exactly right. I'm so sorry about your tragedy. I can't imagine. My dad was very good at teaching me about speed, paying attention to the road and everything around. But, there is a difference it's usually only me in the car. When I'm driving, I'm paying attention to the road like you are right now."

"Me too, but like I said, you have to live life as it's given to you. Appreciate what you have, if you've messed up, ask for forgiveness but you have to move forward. Live a new life, helping those who need help if you can. I love my new husband and baby so much. I totally enjoy helping the ladies at Over the Rainbow, I go there a couple of times a week and lead a bible study. It gives me peace. I try to help the ladies not live in the past. Everyone's life has things in the past that they try to hang on to or it tries to hang on to them. Mine did. And coming here was God's way of helping me find the new path of my life."

Lara looked out her window, concentrating on the green pastures full of cattle and wildflowers, yellow, blue, and red as they passed by. "I have to say that I've been blessed to actually not have at this point in my life, deep regrets. Yes, I wish my parents were here with me but I had a great life with them while they were here on earth with me. I had a relationship with a man that I ended but was blessed that my father had instilled strength in me to stand firm, and I did. I hadn't given him my heart and slammed him out the moment I realized he was after my money and not my heart.

"My dad taught me well and I'll never have that happen again. I was blessed but one thing I know is I'll never risk my heart. So that's why I'm here, to bless people with a great stay while they're here like Pebble did. I get to also have new friends like you and your sisters-in-law. And I like that you work with the home for unwed mothers. I won't be able to do that yet but maybe later I might be able to help."

"I'll tell you that word is already out that you secretly supplied the house with a huge donation. No, don't get upset. One of the young ladies was coming up to the table from behind you and saw you slip that envelope into the large jar. When they found all that money in it, she told them what she'd seen. So, they have realized that you want to be a hidden donator. But I'm letting you know that word is getting out. They may have vowed to keep your secret but it's leaking. I think they do it quietly because they love that you gave it secretly." She winked. "You, Lara, are an inspiration."

Lara didn't know what to think in that moment. "It's just some money that I had and I wanted it to go to them. I admire those who can't keep their baby, but want to provide it a good home with someone who can't have one themselves. So, giving something to help made me happy. And, though I'm not looking for any pats on the back for it, I liked slipping it in. Hopefully everyone who now knows I did it will keep it to themselves. I can just pretend that I don't know anyone knows it."

Abby winked. "You just go on about your business and pretend no one knows it. Now, this town we're going to has a great diner on the lake that I love. We can eat there then go car shopping."

"I like the sound of that." She liked the subject change too.

She sat there quietly and watched the country pass by and she was happy and comfortable. She'd let thoughts of the connection she'd had with Jake not get in her way this week. She'd worked and kept thoughts of him shut down since the weekend. And thankfully he hadn't come around at the times she was normally outside. Then again, she'd altered her time out there so that it wasn't in the evening when he made his rounds, so that could have been some of his not stopping by during his rounds of protecting his town.

And though she was glad they hadn't encountered each other, there was a lingering sense of longing that had dug down deep in her gut when the thoughts snuck up and she pushed them away and focused on her day ahead.

* * *

Jake had gone two weeks without seeing Lara, *busy* weeks hunting for a mountain lion and looking out for his town. All while trying to avoid any more thoughts about the new resident and owner of Sweet Dreams Motel.

He'd begun to stay at the ranch more in the evenings and let the deputies do their work. It meant not passing by Lara's motel, avoiding seeing her sitting outside—he didn't need to crowd her—or tempt himself.

The woman had messed up his sleep habits. He wasn't sleeping enough to have dreams. When he did sleep and a dream did happen, it got him out of bed because he saw the sweet Lara in every dream. And there was no sleep after that so he would get up and go out onto the porch to stare up at the sky. The stars shining down on him usually gave him peace when he was having a hard time. Now, it only gave him the immense, vivid knowledge that he had plans to always sit on this porch alone.

Alone. The simple word now felt like a punch in the gut—or the heart.

He'd never felt this complicated turmoil. So, trying to avoid it in his mind at night, he was working hard every minute he was at the ranch or at work trying to get tired enough to sleep. Nothing had helped last night. There was no sleep. None.

And it was showing today, his day off so he'd gone out to Matt McConnell's ranch and helped round up cattle and then vaccinate them. Matt was a new rancher in town, though the ranch had been sitting there unoccupied for years. Now, Matt was taking it over and rejuvenating it. Helping him out had been a welcome-to-town service and a keep-his-mind-off-Lara option for Jake.

Now, heading home from Matt's ranch, Jake was passing through town because the ranch was on the other side of town, and he was at the stop light. There was a black SUV in front of him and it turned and went down the road toward the Sweet Dreams Motel. The SUV had paper plates instead of metal and shiny clean tires. Jake's gaze followed it as it turned into the motel's entrance, and then he pushed the gas pedal and hooked a left instead of going straight and toward his ranch.

Nope, his mind was on the new vehicle in town. It was a Monday evening, a slow day for the motel, and unable to stop himself, he was slowly driving down the road toward the motel, taking it all in. As he approached the entrance to the motel, he saw Lara. Beautiful, she opened the back door and lifted a pile of packages, turned and shut the door with her hip—the top two toppled from her armload and hit the ground.

Instant reflex took over, Jake yanked the steering wheel and drove into the parking lot, pulled in behind the SUV and was out in an instant. Lara had started to bend down, other boxes wobbled so she'd remained standing, looking at him, startled.

"I'll get it," he said, reaching her, then he bent down and scooped up the two large yellow envelopes. "Sorry you dropped this. I was passing by and saw it happen."

Their gazes were locked.

"Thank you." She gave a nod to her new vehicle. "As you can see, I now have an official vehicle to gather belongings for my business, not that I can carry them all at one time. As you can see I can still drop things as I get out."

He hitched a half smile. "You had an armload. But I like it—the car. I like the SUV." He liked her arms too that were wrapped around the packages—he focused on her face. "Have you been doing good this last couple of weeks?"

"Yes, I've been busy, making some more changes. I had lunch with Abby today and she went vehicle hunting with me. It was nice. She helped me find my new SUV."

"That's great. Friends are worth having. I'm glad you're finding them."

"Me too. I guess you've been busy too."

He nodded. He felt awkward. "Yes, I have. I went and helped a friend round up some cattle and vaccinate them. That's where I was coming back from when I saw this new vehicle. I was behind you without realizing it was you."

"Sheriff Jake doing his job."

"But I was also making sure you were okay. I saw the new tag at the stoplight and saw it was an SUV, then it headed this way and when you turned in I headed this way too. I thought it would be unusual to have a new customer check in this time of day on a slow Monday."

"Thank you for checking. So, how did your roundup go that you were at." She headed toward the door. He followed, still carrying the packages.

"It went great. We helped out a new man in town who has a small herd and he needed them all checked out and vaccinated. Me and a few other ranchers in town went and helped him. Bo is working to get a large order of stirrups out, so couldn't help. And Tru is out of town today for a show. But Jarrod was there with me."

"That was nice. I was with Abby buying my SUV, as I said. They are a great family, I like them very much. And sweet Pops, goodness, what a man." She unlocked the door and went inside.

He followed her inside the motel's office, smelling the soft scent of her hair as he followed her to the counter. She set everything down and he did too, their arms touched, he almost froze but thankfully didn't. He stepped back, locked his hands to his hips, needing to grip something to stop the want to reach out for her.

What was wrong with him and the need to be closer when he was near this woman? He'd stayed away but now it was clear she drew him like a bee to pollen.

CHAPTER TWELVE

Lara had kept her mind off this man and now here he stood. Just that was all it took for her crazy traitorous heart to start pounding like a group of drummers in a loud band. "Do you often help others round up their cattle?" Thankfully the question popped from her chaotic brain.

He held her gaze. "Yes, when they need me, I go. It helps me relax on my day off. Do you relax on your day off—do you have days off? I know you were at the festival but your phone is your attachment to your motel?"

It wasn't any of his business but she realized she didn't care if he knew and it was her being obstinate thinking rudely of his question. "I haven't designated a day off or hired anyone to relieve me yet. I do have a very nice young lady who comes in and cleans the rooms. She worked today while I went looking for my vehicle. And I can book from my phone. I actually like keeping my mind busy, so it's not a problem."

"Same here,' he said, then asked, "What are you doing this evening?"

She hesitated on that. She was doing nothing. She had done nothing but work on book numbers and getting her registration online to help in the future but other than that, nothing much. "I'll work on things, have a quiet evening."

He shifted from one boot to the other. "It's going to be a great evening and…I'm off. I was planning on cooking steak on the pit. Would you want to have a steak out there—just to give you an excuse to leave the motel."

Her heart had dropped to her feet then bounced back up and slammed her in the throat. She coughed and took a moment to swallow to get everything back where it belonged. Go to his house and eat…she needed to say no. *No.* She opened her mouth and said, "Sure. That would be nice. You have a beautiful ranch. Have you seen your eagle lately?" She had wondered about the beautiful bird.

He crossed his muscular arms, drawing her gaze. "He hangs around. After we eat, I could drive you down there, sit on the hill and see if he comes fishing. It's a good time to see him."

Her heart thundered and she pushed the thoughts of saying no away. She liked his ranch and the eagle. Nothing ro…romantic. Nope. Nothing romantic about her thoughts. She just wanted to see the eagle. "That would be nice."

"Okay, I guess if you want to drive your SUV out or want me to come pick you up? I think I know the answer to that."

She smiled, couldn't help it. "I have two vehicles now but I'll test drive my new, large SUV out there today and see how it takes the road."

"Great. How about seven?"

He sounded as hesitant as she did. "Seven sounds perfect." *Heaven* had almost come out of her crazy mouth.

He nodded as he stepped back. "I'll have things

started. Knock on the front door or just come around to the back patio. I have a sidewalk that comes around where I'll be."

"I'll do that. See you then."

He nodded, turned and walked out the door that still stood ajar. Then he closed it and she turned and grabbed hold of the counter with trembling fingers. Her breath caught. What had just happened?

She was going to Jake's home for dinner, that's what happened.

* * *

Jake made it back to the house, and took a very hot shower, trying to burn sanity back into his brain as he let the hot water fry his head and his shoulders. He got out and dressed, feeling a little bit calmer.

He had not intended to ask her over.

Thankfully he had two steaks in the icebox waiting and ready. He always cooked two at a time so that he had one extra to warm up for another meal over the next two days. But he hadn't had anyone over for dinner in—

well, he didn't know how long. He lived a quiet life after work. Him and him alone, unless he was invited to dinner somewhere or unless something was going on in town, a gathering, a meeting, a wedding…or business, making sure everything went on safely.

Normally, he worked. He could cook, thank goodness, so that wasn't a worry. He went to the kitchen and opened the refrigerator and brought out the two steaks that were waiting to go on the outdoor pit. Tonight, the two steaks would get eaten by two people.

He was actually having dinner with someone. The last time he'd cooked for two was when he'd flown down early one morning and spent the day with his mother, then had cooked steaks out on her barbeque pit for them before flying home the following day. That had been seven months ago. His mother traveled as little as he did.

He wondered if his mother had shared a meal with anyone other than him—sure some girlfriends she played tennis with and hung out with, but a date? It was a question he might have to ask her sometime. She needed to step out at some point. He had it on his mind, then he thought about himself but pushed it away. If he thought his mom needed to go out, his brain was telling him *he* needed to do the same. Seeing the beautiful Lara horseback riding through his pastures would be perfect. Taking her to the soft flowing creek in the ravine, where he used to swim in the summers and swing from a rope that to this day still hung from a tree, would be nice. He paused putting salt on the steaks, remembering how he'd had fun having the Monahan brothers over when they weren't herding cattle. Or after a hard day of working cattle. Times they'd still been relaxed teens not knowing what was coming. Them losing their parents, and then almost losing the ranch, but with their hard work and determination the ranch had survived and now they had full lives filled with family.

He'd had family

And lost it when his dad died. His mother was still alive but gone. He had put tie-downs on his life because he felt he had to watch out for her. And he did. He was an adult and a sheriff and he could handle everything. His dad had always said he was tough like him but had the gentle heart of his mother. Right now, as he carried everything out to the outdoor workspace beside his pit, his mind went to Lara. The beauty who had locked her heart away, the heart he was wondering about.

Moments later he had prepared everything and it was near seven. The patio table was set. He'd opened a can of beans and a can of corn, quick and easy additions to his meat of choice when he was home cooking on the grill. When he was cooking for himself. Now, he wished he'd headed to the store and had on hand something special to create to go with the steaks. But he didn't have that to offer her. This was a very plain meal but at least he had a steak and he wasn't taking that for granted. He could cook a steak and so he relaxed.

He was just ready to see her. And that was what had him on edge, not the lack of classy side dishes. Most of the time, whenever he was eating at home, it was out here on the porch alone but tonight he was having company. As he was thinking that, he placed the steaks on the pit. He heard a sound and turned just as she rounded the corner of the stone house. Obviously, he had missed the sound of the SUV or he'd just been too deep in his thoughts of her. He didn't hear her arrive because his brain had been on high alert, thinking about her now and listening to anything going on around him.

She looked just as he'd assumed she would, beautiful. She stopped at the corner of the house, her hand reached out to touch the edge of the stone house. As if to steady herself or maybe turn around and leave. She wore a soft green shirt with her white jeans and sandals. It all fit her well and drew his attention.

"Come on over. I need to ask you how you like your steak cooked. It's good to see you." His words came out sounding stunned and crazy, just like he felt.

She moved forward as hesitant as he felt about the evening. She moved with grace and calmness that was completely not what he was feeling.

"I like mine medium well. I can handle a little pink but no red."

"Sounds like my kind of lady. I like it that way too. I'm not a rare eater but have a ton of friends who do." She was his kind of lady though he hadn't meant to say that. "I wouldn't have judged you if you liked your steak well done."

She chuckled. "I had a friend who only liked it well

done and sometimes they came out burned to a crisp. She'd send it back and tell them if they were as great a chef as she'd heard, they could cook a well-done steak that still had taste and softness."

He grinned. "How did that go."

"She said most of the time the chef took the challenge and took the time to make sure she got a great steak."

"That's great," Lara said. "I've had to sometimes pretend to eat a rare steak—which I just can't handle but don't want to hurt the cook's feelings. So, thanks for asking."

He relaxed. "Glad you're honest with me. You don't ever have to pretend with me. I want you to be yourself. I'm always myself." He wanted it more than— reality slammed into him. He wanted her to be herself around him more than he'd ever wanted anything.

"Okay. I can do that. Although I warn you that sometimes you may not like it. I try to be real and honest. But you know, sometimes real can be tough."

"Yeah, I know that. So, it's nice to know that you're not going to hide behind anything."

She had reached the porch and was now standing only a couple of feet away from him. He pulled the lid down over the barbeque pit. "If I have to be real then I need to tell you that I normally only cook for me. So, we're having canned beans and canned corn. Hope that's okay."

Her lips sprang into a huge, amazing smile. And her blue eyes twinkled. "I love it. I'm not picky. I've lived with much worse than canned beans and corn. It actually sounds good."

They stared at each other. He wasn't exactly sure what he was supposed to be thinking because never had he ever been speechless around anyone. But he was in that instant looking at the woman of his dreams he never realized he was missing out on. Or wanted.

He was a strong single man who had control of his life. But looking at Lara he was off balance. She drew him like nothing ever had before.

CHAPTER THIRTEEN

Lara got her boundaries back up, her sanity actually as she walked over to the edge of the patio where the low-rising stone wall separated the patio from the land. "So, this has been in your family for a long time?" She remembered him saying that. She knew that was a fairly safe subject and she could look at the land instead of him. Because his amazing brown eyes that he had sent feelings surging through her that she wasn't needing. Or wanting. When his gaze had touched her lips briefly her mouth had gone dry and her knees had almost turned to jelly and her heart stumbled. It was something she had never felt before.

"Yes," he said, his voice strong like he was and drew her. "It goes way back. My only memories are of my granddad and my dad. This land digs deep in my heart and I'll always keep it. I don't run a huge herd of cattle, but I run enough. Enough to use the money from the cattle sales to pay for the taxes and the upkeep of the land. I grow certain pastures full of oats that grow well in the winter and supplies the cattle with high protein they need. So my dad and granddad taught me, like they'd been taught, to work to carry on our heritage here, while keeping the people of Wishing Springs safe."

She understood that completely. Unable to stop herself she turned and she sank to sit on the flat stone bench. "My dad, you know I told you he loved Texas. We came from here but left when I was about five. Later, when we came to visit, he showed me where he grew up. It was a small ranch over on the other side of Dallas. Country that comes up quickly and then disappears just as fast. Unlike around here where the countryside shows up and stays with you even out on the highway across rolling hillsides. Beautiful pastures with cattle and horses. My dad's heart didn't follow his parents and the land. His brain always came up with ways to make things better. He was a whiz at math, and mechanics were like lyrics in his mind. Two totally opposite-sounding things but he always said they worked together when he was looking at anything. When he started looking at problems people were having trouble fixing, he instantly started working on it in his thoughts. It was a natural thing to him." She smiled. "By the time he entered college he already had an online business where he helped people figure out problems they were having. He started investing his money early and so I was about five when we moved to New York, where he worked with investors in many ways and bought out businesses that were going down, he fixed them and resold them."

"It sounds like he was a smart man."

"He was, but fun. To him, rebuilding a business or helping people save their business gave him joy. And money to make sure me and my mom never had to worry about anything. He just loved helping people achieve greater things. There had been those investors that recognized my dad's brain was a miracle and started investing with him early on and they all only had great things to say about him when he died. I'm sorry I'm rattling on and talking too much. You get the drift. I admired and loved my dad and mom. My mom homeschooled me and we traveled a lot. Dad always teased her and told her that he traveled with her so he could keep her and not lose her interest." Thoughts of her parents' love sent a yearning through Lara. What would it be like to love someone like that? She stopped talking, and unable to stop herself, she looked over at Jake. He stood at the firepit looking at her.

The man looked good, there was no denying it, and as her heart pounded she tried to find what to say next.

He smiled, then reached for a plate. "It's almost time to eat."

Thank goodness.

He placed the steaks on a plate and set it on the table then pulled her chair out for her. "Have a seat and we'll finally eat."

"It smells delicious." She sat down, and he went inside and returned with the two dishes from the stove. She took her napkin and placed it in her lap, glad to have something to do with her hands.

He joined her at the table and looked at her. "Want to bless it?"

"You bless it." And then without thinking, because it had always been a family habit, she held her hand out. Her dad and her mom had always held her hands as her dad blessed the food.

Now, Jake gently took her fingers in his, bowed his head and prayed. She wasn't a fainter—but his touch as he blessed food almost took her breath away, made her feel like…family.

She had missed this and pushed the emotions away as soon as he let her hand go and they had dinner together. As they ate they talked about the town and whatever came to mind. It was as if she hadn't talked to anyone in a long time, and she actually opened up more to this man. This man she wanted to deny she was attracted to but knew there was no denying it.

Sitting there together, a squirrel suddenly hopped on the rock bench and watched them, its little head and black eyes studying them before it jumped down and headed for a nearby oak tree.

"Sweet," she said. "Do you have little animals

come for dinner often?"

"I see a lot from this porch in the evenings or late at night and in the early morning hours."

"It sounds like you spend a lot of time out here. Do you sit out here late at night and early morning?" She could see him here, but it almost sounded like he had trouble sleeping. As she did.

"Actually, I do. This is the first time in a very long time anyone sat at this table with me."

They stared at each other and she wasn't sure what was going on. Her pulse and the gentle way he looked at her had her not certain what she was going to do. Everything in her always reacted differently when she was near Jake. What are you going to do about it? The question rang out again.

Go home.

"Are you ready to go see an eagle?" He stood up and moved to pull her chair out.

She rose, feeling his closeness and liking the feeling. "Yes, I am."

So much for going home…

She could run for home later. But she and Jake were

going to the lake together and she couldn't resist the pull she felt thinking about taking a ride to the beautiful lake with him.

* * *

Jake drove to the hillside overlooking the lake. The sun was beginning to set across the expanse of water, and it was going to be a gorgeous sunset as the sun shimmered in a reflection on the water where the geese that called the lake home floated calmly. The white clouds would turn to a soft pink, then a blue and orange. It was always unique. The eight geese he was used to seeing on the lake were flowing across the water like they always did, enjoying the beauty of the evening like he was.

He looked over at his guest. She was staring out across the lake with a look of anticipation on her face. He prayed that God would send the eagle to make her day.

"The geese are beautiful." She looked his way, as if she'd heard him, and she met his gaze.

Once again, they stared at each other, he had a

feeling she was just as confused and troubled by the electric surge that raced through him being near her as he was. He wasn't looking for anything other than friendship and she'd made that clear so they were in the same lane.

"They are." *And so are you.* "I don't know about you, but I'll admit that I haven't had dinner with anyone in a very, very long time."

"I haven't either. At least, not with a man. I had lunch with a few friends but that's it. I'm actually a bit of a hermit. I usually stick to myself." She looked back at the lake and he made himself do the same.

A hermit? Yes, she was quiet but to say she was almost a hermit didn't fit.

What was he doing? Trying, wanting to push boundaries he didn't want to push. He wanted to remain single. His mother—*don't live your life for your mother.* His dad's words rang out through his stunned brain.

He heard it loud and clear. His dad had always told him to be kind and mindful and to always do as his mother told him when he was young. It showed respect and love. And he did exactly that, but he was an adult now. Still, after losing his dad, he couldn't stand hurting her more, but he couldn't forget the responsibility of giving his heart to someone and then leaving them behind like his dad had done her, not that he'd chosen that path.

The last thing he wanted to do was hurt her. Or, the woman who fell in love with him. He sighed and raked his hand through his hair, his hat set in the seat between him and Lara. He'd needed something to set a boundary between them so the big Stetson had come into play. Now he needed more space.

"Let's get out," he said, and opened his door. Reaching inside he grabbed his hat and slammed it on his head the moment he was out of the confines of the truck. Lara had blasted out just as fast as he had. He made his way to the tailgate and pulled it down, needing to offer her a place to sit. He would not sit.

"He may not show this evening. If not, I hope that doesn't disappoint you too much."

The sun gleamed across her face in a soft way. Highlighting every delicate feature as her glistening eyes held his. "It's been a wonderful evening. I want to see the eagle but this has been a great time." She spun and stared out at the lake. "Your ranch, Jake, you've done wonderfully here." She placed a hand over her forehead to shade her eyes instead of looking at him again.

He stepped up beside her, focusing on the horizon himself, but feeling the sense of her nearness. "Thanks."

"Jake, you wanting to be an officer of the law, to take care of people, I admire that so very much."

Her words drew his gaze and she was looking at him, sincerity filling her eyes. Every ounce of him tensed. *Okay, she admires me, but could she love me— What are you thinking?*

She looked away. He was a tough man. He had a straight, up-front personality. He looked at everything, tried hard not to let anything slip between him and what he was looking for. And yet, she had somehow, in the very short time they'd known each other, slipped inside his mind and put him in a place he'd never been before.

In that moment she gasped and he yanked his gaze off of her, and there soaring through the sky, was the eagle. His wings were spread wide, his white head down, his gaze on the water. He was looking. Jake was looking too as his gaze slid right back to the beauty standing only a couple of inches away, shoulder to shoulder with him.

"He was probably sitting a long way back," Jake explained. "They have amazing eyesight. He saw something." Just like Jake was seeing something. But the eagle knew what it was looking for and in that moment—Jake knew he was no longer sure if he wanted what he'd always committed himself to. Never falling in love.

Lara gasped again and he yanked his gaze from her to the lake, following her gaze that hadn't left the eagle. In that moment it was diving toward the surface of the lake. Like a bomb heading for its target the eagle slammed headfirst into the water. The geese instantly flew into the sky and away, not waiting for any more excitement.

"Oh no." Lara exclaimed.

"He'll come up." But it didn't.

"He's not," Lara said, her voice frantic.

"It will," he assured her and then its white head

popped through the surface.

"Thank goodness," she stated, her voice serious. "Now, what?"

Jake had never seen an eagle struggling in the water. Not totally struggling, it wasn't going back under and it was moving slowly toward the shore, white head bobbing. "I'm not sure what's wrong. But, it's not drowning. Maybe he's too wet. I've actually never researched that, having never witnessed it before."

His head bobbed in the water, heading toward the far side of the lake, the closest side to the eagle. It reached the two-foot tall shore of weeds, his dark wings waved out as its head dipped and he moved awkwardly into the tall green weeds.

About three feet from the water's edge it stopped. But Jared had seen what it had. He sighed. "He has one of the geese."

"*No*," she said in an exclamatory whisper of dismay.

He nodded. "He had targeted one of the geese, zeroed in and dove. It had no chance but the others did and may never return." He knew it was so. He hated it.

But, the eagle had gotten its dinner.

"I thought it was going after fish."

"Me too. Food for them comes in feathers too. I hate it, but it didn't do anything wrong. I'm sorry you had to see that. Eagles, like other animals, are built to live off the land and produce. He only gets what he needs to eat."

"I understand. It was just a shock to see it. Will the other geese come back? I hope not."

"I'll have to watch and see. They may not come back." He studied the now faint pink sky, seeing no geese mixed in with the soft tones. "They felt safe here, but no more."

She turned toward him. "I bet they come back. One time won't change it. They have to love this lake and well, I can't feel terrible about it. Humans eat ducks and geese, and the eagle has to eat too."

"Right. We have to all do what we have to do to survive." Their gazes were locked, and he felt the thump of his heart as she nodded.

Unable to stop himself he lifted his hand and touched her face. "I'm glad you came out."

"Me too," she said, stepping back. "And it's been a great time, Jake. I really love your ranch. And your cooking. But I've got to go home."

He let his hand drop to his side. "I'll take you there."

And so, they got back inside the truck and within moments they were traveling back the way they'd come. Back to their separation from closeness.

He waved as she drove away moments later in her big SUV. It was crazy how for a few short moments he'd thought he could change the way he believed. But in that moment when that eagle dove down and struck that beautiful bird, he knew he couldn't do that. Like his mother had always said, when it strikes the one you love, it stays in your heart forever. And she didn't want him doing to someone he loved like his dad had done to her.

He knew right then, despite touching her, that he couldn't do that to her. No matter how much he knew, if he let himself, he could want Lara in his life.

CHAPTER FOURTEEN

Lara carried a huge pitcher of sweet tea out the back door of the Over The Rainbow house and out onto the patio. The home for unwed mothers was having a celebration of life today, and she was thankful to be here. She and Lana had met in town earlier in the week and had lunch at one of the small diners away from the wonderful crowd at The Bull Barn. She learned that Lana's mother, Peg Garwood, the founder of the home, had been an unwed teen when she'd gotten pregnant with Lana. Lara loved that Lana had followed in her mother's footsteps by becoming a counselor and joined her mother in devoting her life to helping these unwed mothers. Lana and Peg's story touched her deeply.

They spent their life helping unwed ladies bring

their babies into the world. Then helped them pick a waiting couple for their babies or helped them make the choice to keep their child. Lara loved that. She also knew that Lana knew she'd given an envelope of money at the chip chunking gathering. Abby said one of the ladies saw her do it. But Lana hadn't asked Lara how she was able to give so much, just said they always appreciated donations. Why she'd done it or how, Lana said nothing about.

They seemed happy to have her here in the month that she'd been here in this wonderful town making a life for herself. Today, she and Lana and her other friends, the Monahan ladies, were giving this party for all the women at Over The Rainbow.

There were nine pregnant young women here right now. Including Vivian, who cleaned rooms at the motel. They'd put picnic tables out on the lawn and Lana and Peg had taken the ladies shopping. They'd gotten another donation from Lara, though she didn't put her name on it, she knew they suspected it was her. She'd asked in the note to take the mothers shopping for new clothing for themselves to celebrate this day and the fact that they'd chosen life for their child. Just the idea of what she was able to do pleased her heart. Looking around at the young women in different stages of pregnancy with their new outfits on, their new shoes to go with the hairstyles and manicures that Clara Lyn and Reba always supplied them with for free, it made Lara's heart swell with a kind of joy she'd never felt before. These ladies were about to bring life and happiness into the world. And she was able to help reward them for that wonderful decision they had made.

She set the tea on the table with all the other containers of drinks. "Here you go," she said to Lana.

Lana smiled at her. "It looks like we're having an Easter party with the wonderful new and colorful outfits the ladies bought. I'm telling you they were so excited to go shopping yesterday. Most of these ladies don't have a lot of money and we get donations all the time but we've never had one specifically that said go buy something frilly and beautiful to wear in your honor for this celebration. Lara, that was a thoughtful gift."

"You are very nice *implying* it was me. I know one of them saw me give the envelope at the chip toss. but no one saw me give this. I'm just glad the ladies look happy. And that makes me happy."

"You know I know."

She gave her a nod. "It's between us, me, you, and your mom. I'm assuming she knows too. These gals need to just think they got a donation but have no idea it was me, right?"

"Exactly right. Our mouths are shut. As a matter of fact, I had suspected word would get out but if anyone else knows they're keeping it to themselves too."

"For that I am thankful and it shows me that I made the right choice coming to Wishing Springs."

They smiled at each other just as Pebble came walking over. The small beautiful older lady had a spring to her step and a smile on her face as she looked at them with her sparkling sapphire eyes. She'd looked happy ever since selling the motel to Lara, and she was happy too.

"This is a great day. A celebration I never even thought to have here but this celebration of life is sweet and touching and so very well deserved. Each of these ladies made a decision that might have been so hard for them. Complicated and hard but oh so right. And to see them smiling and happy is wonderful. Now, what are we going to do?"

"The gals are going to have a delicious meal donated by The Bull Barn, our favorite chef prepared it and sent it over. Bo and Pops made sure it got here. It's all set up and ready. Now, Maggie is going to give us a devotional talk about new life, new beginnings, and making new dreams for ourselves." Lara smiled. "Everyone is included, like you, Pebble. From what I hear you have made a huge dream come true."

Pebble beamed and put her wedding band wearing left hand to her heart. "I made the best decision of my life when I married Rand. We both went through a life of joy and pain and now we're making our new life together. Dreams are wonderful. I hope both of you ladies are doing some of that too."

Pebble's eyes rested on Lana and then on Lara and her heart rattled. Her pulse shook as she thought about it. About how since dinner with Jake they had both distanced themselves. She'd known standing there on that hillside watching the eagle that something deep had rang between them. She knew that, just like her, he wasn't looking for that.

But still, whether she wanted to or not she thought about it. The overwhelming want to take a step forward and find out what his arms would feel like around her. His kiss—not where she wanted to go. But she had, just like her thoughts had gone every night since that evening.

She looked at the ladies. "It's been a great day and I'm enjoying myself. This is where I belong. And I have wonderful reviews on the motel. I had thought about changing the name to the Sweet Dreams Inn, and it is an inn to me, but it's known as a motel and that's okay. Motel brings in a downhome feel and keeps me from being overly fancy. I think that brings everyone in."

Pebble lightly patted her arm. "Well, I like what you said, but like I told you before, change it if you want to. I'm agreeing with you, though that motel fits. It's not too flamboyant, not overdone, just simple and inviting. I'm glad to know my motel has a history."

"And yes, it does. Everyone, when they come in, tell me they are glad I'm carrying it on because they love coming to Wishing Springs and staying at the Sweet

Dreams. They eat out at The Bull Barn or one of our other small but awesome diners and go shopping down Main Street. It's just wonderful the festivals y'all hold to draw people in—including the chip throwing." She chuckled. "Sometimes, I don't have enough rooms to fit everyone. I'm already booked and have been four weeks out. So, I've been thinking about enlarging the motel."

"Really," Lana was the first to speak.

Pebble was smiling and Lara suddenly had a feeling she was on the right track. "Pebble, had you thought about enlarging the motel? I mean, it's got that property on the side and then extends to the back some too. It would hold another section of cabins."

The sweet lady's smile widened. "Actually, I had thought about it. My sweet Cecil, my first husband, bought the extra land in case we wanted to enlarge but then I lost him and decided not to. I probably wasn't going to hang on to the motel that long. I needed a way to start a new life if I decided it was time. It would have put more stress on me than I needed. Especially with me worried about Rand, my sweet new husband." She smiled and it touched Lara's heart. "But, all that land was included in your buy, Lara, so you have my blessing. If you have your sights on something bigger, go for it."

Clara Lyn had just walked up with Reba trailing her. "What are you going to do? What are you going to do?" she rattled the repeated question out, excitement glowing in her expression as the bracelets' sang their tune on her moving hands.

Lara laughed. "I'm going to enlarge the Sweet Dreams Motel."

Reba hustled up. "Oh, my goodness. With all the different things we have going on now, since the *Gotta Have Hope* column drew attention to our town, we need a better—no can't get better, just bigger motel. Enlarging is perfect. Sweet Dreams Motel has a great reputation and people come to just stay there too, so you sweet Lara, are on the right track." She finally stopped rambling.

Lara was smiling at her enthusiasm and felt satisfaction. "I'm very glad because I'm going to get the process going. It would also let me employ more help. Vivian does a fantastic job and I love being able to give her that opportunity while she is here in our town. And like Reba pointed out so well, we have a lot drawing people here now. Chip throwing of all things." Everyone laughed. "That so many people would drive to watch and then drive out because there was no place to stay made me think strongly about it." That and needing something to occupy the fact that the handsome sheriff was taking over her thoughts and she'd needed something to push him away. "There are people calling for rooms and asking me what's happening next."

Pebble looked pleased. "Yes, I love it and I knew when I chose you that I chose right. God led you here and you have a plan just like God's got a plan—don't forget that." Her voice rose in a singing tone as her eyes sparkled. "Plans meet sometimes. Destinies meet and we all get to watch."

Lana took over the conversation, much to Lara's relief. "I agree with everything but now it's time to get these ladies over here and have a party. A celebration of life with gifts, our sweet Maggie Hope is going to talk."

They headed that way intent on getting the celebration started and Lara knew that exactly what she'd been thinking about was right, it was time to make the Sweet Dreams Motel into a larger place and build on that. The more people she could help draw to this inviting town the more benefit it would be to everyone, but especially this wonderful home for unwed mothers. A mission also that she could be looking for. Opportunity to be a giver and not a taker.

She had thoughts of Jake in that moment. He was a giver. He was giving up his chance at love and a family in order to give peace to his mom and the woman out there who could fall for him. The many women out there who could fall for the amazing man. He was giving it all up for his mother and this wonderful town of Wishing Springs. And that thought had not left her.

It clung to her. She went to sleep every night with it drilling into her. Jake Morgan was a strong, loving cowboy. The best man she had ever known. Yes, her dad would be telling her to take him out of the equation because this was about something different from a father's love, and she knew that. She felt this was a love like she'd witnessed between her parents.

Jake Morgan was a godly man, and she—no, she wasn't putting her name in the slot, but some woman out there was going to miss out on loving him.

CHAPTER FIFTEEN

Jake had gotten a call from Matt McConnell, the new cowboy in town, he'd found paw prints. Thankfully not a dead cow but prints. Jake headed that way, pulled up into the drive, and got out. Matt stood there beside his truck waiting, a grim look on his face.

"Thanks for coming, Jake. Hop in and I'll take you out there. I was repairing a fence in the back pasture and found the paw prints on the other side of the creek. They're coming out and heading off my property. I'm not talking about cat prints, they're bigger than that."

Jake climbed into the passenger side of the large truck. Matt hadn't come into town much since moving here. He'd said after he got settled in that he would, but right now he was getting his ranch going and keeping to himself. Jarrod had met him and gotten them all out to help with his cattle as a welcoming committee. The ranch had been in Matt's family for generations but hadn't actually had one of the family living on it for years. Until now.

He looked at Matt, the cowboy had a confident look about him, telling Jake that this incident hadn't scared him. Just put him on alert, as it should. "I hate you got this kind of a welcome to our area, but thank goodness you didn't find a dead cow or anything else. But yes, we have been having incidents. The Monahan Ranch had one a couple of weeks ago and before that another ranch, both with a cow dead. So, we do have a mountain lion roaming. At this point no one has been injured and I'm thankful for that. As you probably know they travel a large territory so I have a feeling this might be the same one that was reported in another county. You said he was leaving your property?"

"He was going," Matt said. "You'll see his paw prints leaving through the fence line. This ranch is only few thousand acres, not much compared to the Monahan Ranch here or my family ranch near Corpus Christy

Bay. This one is easily crossable compared to all of those."

Matt was part of the huge ranch in South Texas. This cowboy knew his business, and Jake wasn't sure if he was here just to update the property or permanently. "I didn't ask you when we were all out here working, are you making this your home property?"

"I love our coastal ranch," he gave Jake a grin. "I'm very proud of all my heritage and feel the need to build these up. But my name is McConnell and proud of that. I'm glad to be a part of the Texas group of ranchers whose names start with M." He hitched a brow.

Jake gave a short laugh. "There does seem to be a lot of ranchers whose last names start with M. Mine included. We're glad to have you. Your family has a great reputation, like most of the M names do. At least the ones I know, the Monahan's and the McIntyre's and mine, the Morgan's and yours the McConnell's."

Matt gave a nod. "It's a little funny actually. I come from the Rayburns and the Pearls on my grandmother's side of the family. It's all connected now in the McConnell name but history goes way back in my family. Our land is spread all over Texas. The Rayburn land was this and also out toward the Trinity River in the Midway area. I came from ancestors who had the urge to roam, so they did and ended up in Star Gazer and down the line it gets complicated." He finally smiled. "My brothers and my dad are firm lovers of the ranch there. But, like my great- great-grandfather Treb Rayburn had the need to roam, it's been in my blood too. So, now, my need to spread my wings got the better of me and here I am. I love my family, have a great family so don't take that wrong."

Jake gave him a look. "I get it. It sounds good to have so much past and a big family. I come from a small family and only have my mother left. But she took off to Florida after we lost my dad. And like you love yours from a long way off, I love her too. But she's not coming back here, I have to go see her and I always will do that." And he would. His mother meant the world to him…he shut his thoughts down as he instantly thought of Lara.

"You obviously haven't done a background check on the new man in town," Matt said. "You would have seen my family."

He was right. "I usually check newcomers out but I'll admit I had other things on my mind and you didn't alert me by any conduct that I needed to act on." Jake didn't say he had had a woman on his mind instead of business.

A woman who was still hanging out in his mind and taking him away from where his thoughts needed to be. This was proof he'd dropped the ball on protecting the town.

But the woman, no matter how hard he tried, Jake couldn't lose her in his thoughts.

"It's right up here over the hill," Matt said, interrupting Jake's runaway thoughts.

They'd crossed a couple of cattle guards over the land and now they drove up a hill and he looked down the hill to the creek at the base, the fence was across the water. Matt parked and they climbed out and walked to the edge of the creek..

Jake's eyes were on the thin crossing as they reached the edge and he saw the paw prints clearly marked in the mud on the other side. He walked a few feet down and stepped from the muddy land to the rock and over to the other side as Matt did the same.

When Jake took the short steps to the paw prints he knelt down, keeping his knee off the mud as he studied the print. "I'm glad you called me and that it's June and dry, and the prints are not washed away by rain." He had kept talking but knew he'd lost track of time because his thoughts hadn't been completely where they should have been. His thoughts kept sidetracking to Lara, but finally they were on these paw prints.

He'd tried to stay away from her as much as possible. But it boggled his mind in that moment that he was acting like a chicken. He wasn't one but at that moment he felt like it.

He pulled his phone out and did his job, took a photo of the five clear footprints that emerged from the water and headed to the fence not too far from the edge of the stream. Thankfully the odd fence line had hindered any cattle from coming over and walking over the paw prints as they disappeared on the other side of the barbed wire fence and the overgrown pasture next door. But he'd left prints behind. Big prints.

Jake stood up. "He came from across your property

and heading that way. Since you're on the edge of our county line, he seems to be heading to another area."

"I thought so too. Before I called I had brought my four-wheeler down here and drove down the creek through several acres of my land in search of other prints and found none. This creek crosses off my land not too far through those trees up ahead. I called right after looking. I also have no dead animals, they're all accounted for. Have you heard of any other killings around me?"

"Yes, the Monahan ranch is near here, you're on the end of their ranch, down past where Jarrod lives. I'm thinking that means he's heading away from us. Which for us is good, hopefully we won't have any more cattle down. I'll call the next county and warn them to be on the lookout." He was relieved at the thought that the mountain lion was leaving his county. It was a relief that no one was hurt and the few cattle lost would stop.

Matt's brows met. "They travel a huge area on a regular basis, but it's a lot of ground to cover. From those paw prints, it's easy to see he's not a baby but an adult. I'm assuming it's a male. And no baby prints so

I'm thinking it's not a mom. I'm not a pro when it comes to mountain lions, just read a little about it in the moments since finding these prints. They're loners."

Jake felt what he just said like it was a strike to his heart. "I don't want him lookin' for love and bringing up a family near our town, so I'm fine with that."

Matt looked at him with dim eyes. "Yeah, I don't know about you, but I'm a loner too. Me and this land will be just fine all by ourselves."

"Same." Jake said firmly, but knew he wasn't feeling it like before, whether he wanted to or not, Lara's sweet face came to mind.

But, the question came to his officer mind, what was pushing the new cowboy in town to be a loner?

They'd crossed back over the creek and headed back to the truck, climbed inside, and Jake found Matt looking at him as he cranked the engine.

"So, you're not looking to fall in love?" Matt asked.

"I wasn't expecting you to ask me that question but the honest answer is no, I'm not. I'm the sheriff and I have a responsibility to everyone."

"Yeah, I get it. Me, I'm here to be free." Matt

looked ahead as he pressed the gas and they headed in a round circle before going back the way they'd come.

"Well I hope you find your freedom here." Jake wondered what Matt was trying to be free from. Jake understood that, he was trying to be free too but he wasn't.

It hit him hard that he'd been trying to stay away from every common place you could normally find him. No lunch at The Bull Barn lately. He was trying to avoid the woman who wouldn't leave his mind. Or his heart.

So that left him with, thankfully, hunting for a wild cat. That was an odd thing to be grateful for but he was.

* * *

"So, nothing's going on between those two," Clara Lyn said with a sigh when her and Reba had arrived at work and were getting ready for their clients. "I tell you, either she's been working and he's been working, so maybe it's just the timing is wrong."

Reba looked over her shoulder with a disgruntled look on her face. "I just don't get it. They are meant for each other as far as I can tell. Young love, yes, they're both mid-thirties but still. They're missing out and I know that Jake's mother would be uneasy if her son fell in love. But you saw them yesterday at church and you said they hadn't seen each other lately. I was watching and their gazes met across the room and it was like they both had a big bucket of ice-cold water tossed on them—or hot, scalding water. They both looked panicked. They tried to hide it but I saw it as they both instantly slid into the pews on opposite sides of the church. Since I was sitting towards the back I could see them. Yep, I know you always sit at the front, Clara Lyn, but you missed the show. That's why I sit toward the back, so I can see everything that happens."

Clara Lyn slapped her hand on her hips sending all her bracelets to jingling. "I know I keep saying I'm going to sit back there too, so I don't miss things but if I start moving backward the preacher is going to wonder why I'm slinking to the back. He might think I have something going on. Or that I don't like him anymore."

Reba busted out laughing. "Yeah, girl, you and me both. I remember when we were both younger and we were looking for love. We looked in all the wrong places."

Clara Lyn gave a huff of a laugh. "Boy, did we. Still, God worked it out for both of us. It's just got to work out for them. And they're not looking in all the wrong places like we did. They're not looking in any places and that's the problem."

Reba picked up a towel then laid it back down. "Is there anything we can do? You know, like fix them up or lock them in a room together." She laughed. "Not really but there has to be something."

"I'm thinking," Clara Lyn muttered as her mind rolled. "What about if we write a letter to *Gotta Have Hope*. I mean, you know, we don't have to say who we are or mention them. We could just talk about having hesitations and problems."

Reba's face lit up. "That sounds good."

Clara Lyn was ready. "We could put a hopeful name on it like they do then we can drive somewhere and drop it in the mail so it won't tell them we're from here."

"Great idea. We can take a drive within a hundred

miles and pop it into a mailbox. There's a lot of people within a hundred-mile radius around us."

"I think that's a great idea. Okay, we have customers coming now, so tonight before we head home we're going to write it and get it in the mail sometime this week." Clara Lyn zeroed in on Reba. "Be thinking about what we should write, *but* do *not* be talking about it."

Reba slapped her hand on her leg. "I certainly wouldn't talk about something this important. I want our sweet cowboy sheriff to have a wonderful life. Not a single life out there on that ranch all by his lonesome. Don't want Lara alone either. Something is going on with her, don't you have that feeling."

"I do. And you know you and I have so many customers that we usually know when something is wrong. We've gotten to learn their movements, and something in Lara Strong's background is hitting her hard, holding her back. We're not going to investigate that but I would like to know what it is. But if we dug up something bad, no, we're just going to knock that out of the way and what will be will be."

"I'm with you, girlfriend. We're going to make a change and hope for the best."

Clara Lyn sighed as the door opened and in walked Nurse Bertha Lee. They'd gotten finished talking just in time. They didn't need Bertha knowing and telling them to butt out.

CHAPTER SIXTEEN

After a long week of frustration and a mind that refused to shut down with thoughts of Jake, Lara chose her fast two-seater today. She needed to feel the roar of the powerful car that her dad had loved. Needed something to fire up her low feelings as she headed to The Bull Barn to have lunch with the ladies. It had been a long couple of weeks.

Unable to stop herself, her mind had been fluctuating between how much she enjoyed her life here but also she was having trouble seeing so many happy couples here. Like the Monahan ladies. Maggie, Abby, and Cassidy. They all seemed to be so happily married. They'd all had problems but still had love. That had been eating away at her the last few nights. She'd looked up Maggie's articles and been reading all of them, reminding herself that she wasn't alone in her hurts and heartache. Everyone had them. Maggie offered help too, so many that Lara had been tempted to write but had held back. What would she write? What if someone figured out it was her? So no, she'd done as she always did, kept it inside. But still, the article that came out yesterday was on her mind and wouldn't go away. It had been interesting...almost what she might have written in some ways.

It had been from a lady in a small Texas town who was having trouble starting over. She was struggling and she hadn't told anyone in her town why she was hurting. The name of the lady was *Hurting In Texas*, as Lara read the article it struck a chord with her. It seemed like whoever this woman was had trouble being herself. Trouble stepping fully into the light, the life she wanted. She hadn't said what her background was, hadn't stated it in the newspaper, but clearly she was struggling to not fall in love. She just couldn't put herself out there, couldn't risk falling in love though there was someone in town she felt she could give her heart to...if she could take the risk.

Lara had read and reread that post. It was so odd reading that heartfelt note *Hurting In Texas* had written. The letter was different from most of the letters Maggie answered, but it spoke to Lara.

Lara was in a small town hiding her pain—she stopped what she was thinking—she wasn't in pain. *Yes,* she'd lost her parents. She'd also tossed the jerk who'd tried to make her fall for him to get to her parents. *Yes,* she'd had struggles but she had overcome all of them with God's help.

Hadn't she?

That question raged through her as she drove to the stop light at the center of Wishing Springs, on the way to The Bull Barn.

The diner was on the outskirts of town and that was good, because her mind kept thinking about that article. She needed to drive and that was why she'd chosen her car. She was also unable to stop thinking about Jake.

And as she headed through town she actually saw Jake in his sheriff's SUV sitting at a stop sign as she passed by in her convertible. Today she had the top down, needing the wind and the fresh air and the feel as she drove. She knew many people bought convertibles just for that fact. It freed the mind in a way she needed.

But right now, it also exposed her.

It made her clear to people as she drove by. She tried not to look at him but could see out of her side mirror that he was watching her as she drove by at the slow in-town speed limit. Part of her thoughts about him were always, was he safe? What was he doing?

She told herself over and over he wasn't hers to worry about.

But still she'd wondered…wondered if he would be safe—that wonder alone told her she needed to stay away.

She'd heard rumors that he'd been hunting a mountain lion. *That* worried her for the man. She looked in her rearview mirror and saw that Jake had turned onto the road behind her, not close but still there was no vehicle between him and her. No obstacles like there was in life—in her struggling heart.

She tried not to look in the rearview or go over the speed limit as she drove out of town, around the curve and then onto The Bull Barns driveway.

He was still there, and of course, he turned in behind her.

Him coming in behind her had nothing to do with her.

He had distanced himself as much as she had. They both followed the rules that they'd clarified early on since she'd arrived in town.

Now, she drove to the empty spot on the right side of the rocky parking lot. She put the car in park, pushed the button and waited for the top to come from behind and close over her. Then, sucking in a breath, trying to calm her pulse, she got out of the car just as he finished backing his SUV into the only other vacant space across the white rocks from her.

Speak the voice in her head commanded as she stepped out from beside her car as he got out of his SUV, then stepped up beside her. She focused on the rocks and each step, very aware of the man beside her and she said, "I guess you have a lunch group meeting."

"I do. There's a group of us. The Monahan brothers and our new neighbor, Matt McConnell. Are you having lunch with someone?"

Her pulse raced at just the sound of his voice. "I am. The ladies, they asked me to come. You know, the normal crowd. Clara Lyn, Reba, the Monahan ladies, and Lana from Over The Rainbow."

"Great group. You and Lana seem to have become friends. Everyone keeps talking about how hard it is to keep your names separated, Lana and Lara."

She looked at him and saw his smile as they continued walking, neither of them walking fast. "Yes, we laugh at the confusion sometimes they are so close. But now I have a friend, Lana is a great person and I think she and her mother are doing a wonderful thing with their home for unwed mothers." They'd almost reached the porch and she felt torn between sad and thankful to put space between them.

He stopped walking and she stopped too. "I'm glad you've made friends. Lana sounds like she could be a close friend. As I think everyone in this town agrees, Lana and her mother Peg have an everlasting giving gift. Peg chose life for her child, who grew up and joined her in her mission to help women and babies. They have a great mission. You're doing good too with how you help out."

Her heart pounded looking at him, she shook her head. "Not like they do."

"I've been thinking about what you said about buying the motel and I know who you really are. Know you can do it and it's a good thing for you, I hope. Knowing you could travel the world if you wanted with no worries holding you back. But you chose this town, and so far have helped people come to the motel and have a good stay, but more, you're giving back. Putting money where it makes a difference. I've heard everyone talking about the fact that someone paid for a great shopping day for the ladies from the home."

"It was a great day. Maggie gave a wonderful talk about new beginnings and gifts of love and life. New starts. Anyway, it was a wonderful day and the ladies all celebrated. It made me happy." There she'd move the conversation away from her, about what he suspected she'd done and she put it back on track.

But his eyes on her told her he knew the truth. And the fact that he respected that made her heart thunder louder than it had been.

"I hear you," he said, his voice gentle. "The lady who could do whatever she wanted to in life and chose to buy the Sweet Dreams Motel and make a life here helping others in small ways. I'm sure in life-changing ways that no one will ever know."

She took his words, he'd read her heart. Her plans to make a difference and her heart stumbled. Yes, she had told him why she was here and had been glad about it but lately even adding onto the motel didn't feel right.

She felt left out of her own plan. "Thanks, I needed that. Now, I need to go inside. They'll all be waiting." And watching, and if she walked in with Jake, she might up the rumors—

He moved up the steps and pushed the door open. And there went trying to hide that they'd arrived together.

She knew they were in different vehicles and she could verify that so she passed in front of him, got a strong scent of his aftershave and almost stopped. Thank goodness she didn't because Big Shorty was standing there looking straight at her.

"Afternoon, you two sitting together?"

"No, no, we ran into each other in the parking lot." Her voice didn't sound right.

Jake passed on by her. "I'm having lunch with the men and I see them. Enjoy lunch, Lara."

Stunned that he'd passed on by, she watched him walk away, his voice ringing in her ears. *Stop watching.*

She looked at Big Shorty, grinning Big Shorty. "I'm here for the ladies' group. Thankfully on the other side of the dining room." *Oh goodness, I said that last part out loud too.*

Big Shorty grinned wider. "Follow me. I felt for you and set their table away from the fellas. It's a busy day so that gives you some more distance away from that cowboy. You look a little off balance."

She looked at the big man, he acted like he knew what was going on. "I'm grateful. I am off balance." There she'd said the truth.

"Well hang on, you're doing good." With that he led her across the diner—or started. Doobie and Doonie and Rand sat at a table between her and the ladies. They were all smiling and she smiled back as she went to pass by Rand.

But Rand placed a hand on her arm, stopping her. "I'm letting my wife sit over there with you, because I want her to get whatever she wants out of life. She said you let her start a new life with me when you bought that pretty motel, so I'm thankful to you. I sure hope you're happy. I hope you find love. Real love." His startling words shot through her as his gaze shot across the room and she followed them to Jake.

She yanked her gaze away and found Doobie and Doonie grinning widely. One of them, she wasn't sure which one, patted his hand on the table. "Yep, there's an interesting letter to *Gotta Have Hope* we all read. Did you read it—or write it?"

Write it? Her knees went weak. "*No*, I mean I read Maggie's article like I always do, but I've never written to her."

The other brother, Doobie or Doonie, took over. "It's odd she lives only about a hundred miles away. It's interesting that's an easy drive to a mailbox if you don't want anyone to know it came from here."

Why were they even thinking she might have

written it? "She always has great answers to readers' questions. Why in the world would y'all be looking at me like that?"

She didn't get it. Yes, she felt close to what that letter said, but no one in this town knew that.

Rand raised his hand. "Leave the lady be. You go on and eat lunch and forget what these two said."

She did just that. She was confused as Big Shorty pulled the empty chair out beside Clara Lyn.

"Thanks," Lara said as she sank into the chair, wanting to run out the door. What was going on?

Jangling bracelets' brought her focus back as Clara Lyn tapped her knee. "I'm so glad you joined us."

Big Shorty laid the menu in front of her and she looked up at the big man. He winked, then walked away.

Across the seat from her was Pebble and she realized from where the sweet lady sat, she had a view of Lara and of her husband sitting a few tables over. They were still considered newlyweds, only having been married six or seven months maybe. Rand's sweet words were touching. He loved this lady deeply it was apparent. Now she was looking at Lara with eyes that seemed to dig into her heart.

What was going on?

* * *

Jake tried not to look toward the table where the tense but beautiful Lara sat. All of his instincts told him something was up. But what? What had he missed? Yes, there was tension between the two of them, but she was with the ladies. He couldn't see her face just her profile from where he sat at the head of the table facing the table across the room where she sat. She was the last one on the table of six so seeing her face was hard.

And the ladies kept leaning forward as they talked to her excitedly. He told himself to stop looking but he didn't tell himself soon enough as he realized all eyes at his table were on him.

Jarrod hitched a brow. Matt cocked his head to the side and studied him from the left side of the table. Bo and Tru sitting on the right side of the table just stared, waiting. All of them were waiting.

He looked from one side of the table to the other.

"What do I not know?"

"Well," Jarrod continued. "You are the sheriff and we figured you knew and saw everything. But we see that you don't know something very important."

"I thought something was up when you came out to my ranch to look at the paw prints," Matt said. "You were there, but you weren't there. I asked the guys about it, and they explained it to me what was going on, and now I clearly see it."

He had a bad feeling. "What?"

Bo reached out and laid a hand on the table, "You, buddy—" Then plopped his thumb toward the table across the diner. Only the ones at his table could see the thumb and Jake instantly knew he was pointing at Lara. "...have the look of *love,*" Bo continued to the tune of an old song.

Jake was floored by that, even more floored when Tru—*Tru* Monahan extraordinaire said, "Don't deny it. I've been there. Sometimes we know and sometimes it takes a little shaking up to get it through."

"Okay, you fellas are wrong. I don't know where you got that idea but I'm not in love. I'm not planning on falling in love. It's *not* happening. Y'all know that. I decided that a long time ago and I'm not backing down. I'm giving my sweet mother a heartache, thinking she's going to lose me too. But worse she worries I'm going to break another woman's heart like hers was." There he'd let out his mother's fear.

Tru had looked away but now he met Jake's gaze. "*Sheriff*, cowboy, tough man. Your mother cannot set the timeline of your heart. Yes, you love her. You love her more than anything other than that woman you've given your heart to over there. You can deny it all you want but we know you. Matt came here and he doesn't know you anywhere near as well as we do, but as soon as we pointed it out he saw it—don't look shocked. Yes, we've been gossiping. We are the gossiping cowboys of Wishing Springs."

Everyone at the table grinned but Jake did not grin.

"Yeah," Matt added. "You said you were studying those paw prints but your mind went elsewhere half the time and I saw it."

"We saw it too," Bo said. "Something happened the moment Lara arrived in town and met you. Everyone in town sees it. What's up with all of this? Is it just that you can't see it, or that you're such a protector that you can't be truthful with yourself? Because you're trying to protect your mother's heart?"

"I guarantee you," Tru added. "If you call that sweet mother of yours and you told her what you're feeling and denying, she would tell you to go for it."

He thought about his mother. Remembered all the times she told him how much she loved his dad. And how much it had hurt her that he was dead…she had cried. She'd tried not to but it happened. "I can't do that to my mother. She's already lost one man she loves because of his job."

"This isn't about your job. You're just a man," Bo said, staring with compassion. "Believe me I have a wife who lost the man she loved and it's hard to live through. So, I'm not your mother but I've watched the lady I love go through tough heartache. But in the end my love won. My love helped her. Jake, I don't know what the woman you love has been through. I don't know what's stopping you from accepting that beautiful woman, but most importantly the loving, giving woman we've all watched since she arrived, has your heart. You need to open up and realize you're just a man. Your job is protecting this town, this county. But we, as your friends, find our job is protecting you. And if like Matt said, when you were out there at his place just looking for a mountain lion, you were distracted. And when you were at our place looking at the dead cow that day, we saw you were distracted. A distracted sheriff is not good. So, we're not just here telling you this because we're your friends. We're telling you this because we respect your judgment. And right now, it's off."

The words struck him like a powerful lightning bolt. He scanned the faces looking at him from the men at the table. The four men, and he saw their gazes were all the same, they were concerned about him. And his job. His job that meant everything to him.

"I would not mess up," he snapped. "My job is my life—" Then his gaze locked on Lara as she leaned forward with shock on her face as she talked with the ladies.

Lara…and then his heart thundered with the truth…

CHAPTER SEVENTEEN

Lara stared at the ladies, they'd just told her that she *loved* their sheriff.

"Ladies, I don't know how you've gotten that on your mind, but I am my own person. I'm not going to let love have a hold on me—" she said, leaning forward determined to get their attention, but her gaze slid to Jake... Jake looking at the four cowboys staring straight at him. He looked flabbergasted, in shock. Almost what she was feeling.

She wanted to know why he had that look on his face. Why the man that she admired with all of her heart, the strong man, the man she figured could save the world if he put his mind to it. Or something drove him to it, or someone needed him... *Why* did he have that look on his face?

"See there," Clara Lyn said softly beside her. "You're looking at him. And you love him. Now that article in the newspaper did it say what you are feeling?"

She leaned back in her chair and met Clara Lyn's gaze. "What is it about that letter? I didn't write that letter."

Maggie reached out and tapped the table with long fingernails. "I told you ladies that she didn't write that letter. I knew it wasn't her. It had an unusual sound to it, not her voice. And my answer, as you all read," she paused, her gaze touching Lara's. "I wrote my answer as I always do, to help anyone who might need to hear what God put on my heart to say. That's what I always do. What did I say, Lara?" she asked, her eyes locked on Lara.

Lara was stunned. Everything in her was doing somersaults, doing backward flips' off the edge of a cliff. "You said, sometimes you have to forget everything and do what feels right. Do what deep down in your heart and soul you want to do." Her heart thundered. "You said you have to take that and go with it, if it's safe and doesn't hurt anyone. But the person inside you that's telling you to be weak has to go."

Reba gasped. "You said that word for word. I read it over and over again and I'm sure it was word for word."

She too had read the answer over and over. Let it sink in and was trying to ignore the way it affected her. "Look, y'all, I lost my mother and father in a plane crash. Just like those three cowboys over there that y'all love lost their parents. I loved them with all of my heart. I lived my whole life surrounded by them. Homeschooled, on the road with money that we could have done whatever we wanted to do. My dad moved us to New York and he built a life there helping others make their dreams come true. He invested in people and great ideas. And I tried to do what he wanted by helping him. But then the plane crashed, and in an instant took them away. And I'd already learned the hard way that money can't buy you love, it can buy you creeps looking for money, not love—thank goodness I got that figured out and kicked that one to the side of the road and locked my heart up for safety. Now, here I am sitting here at this table with all of you looking at me like I have to take a chance. A real chance different from the first wrong thought…" She closed her eyes and shook her head. "I can't lose love like theirs—I can't risk knowing love like theirs—"

She pushed her chair back needing space. "I love this town and I love all of you but you have to back off. You have to leave me alone." And then she turned and strode through the diner, out the door and nearly raced to her car.

Inside she was steaming. Every ounce of her was so angry. How could those nice people try to tell her what she didn't want to do? And yet as she slid into her car, slid the key into the ignition, slammed a finger to the button that had the top moving out of her way and letting the sunshine in, she backed up. Thank goodness she'd glanced and no one was in her way. And then she turned and drove out of the parking lot. Making the choice at the road to hang a left heading away from town.

She stomped that gas pedal to the floor and she drove.

She watched her speed. Her dad had taught her to

always watch her speed, especially when she was upset or angry. Take control of her driving and *her life*. So now, she concentrated on the road as she'd put the pedal to the floor and shot to sixty-five, the speed limit, in a very short few seconds. Tears welled in her eyes as the wind surrounded her and she concentrated on what was ahead of her and around her. Speed made her take her mind off what was bothering her aching heart. On this road she watched for deer, animals that could run out in front of her and cows that could get out of broken fences. A broken fence and a hurting heart with a speeding car didn't mix well. Her father's words rang in her ears so she concentrated and glanced at her speed. She was not speeding but she slowed just a little. Control was what she needed.

She had to put her attention on the road.

Her gaze went from one side of the road ahead of her as her heart thundered. She gripped that steering wheel and she cried, slowing slightly and in that moment, she heard a siren blasting.

She looked in the mirror and saw the one man she wasn't ready to see. She saw the heroic, amazing sheriff Jake Morgan. And there was not a look of joy on his face as his siren blared, flashing lights, and out the window he shot his hand to the side demanding she pull over.

She pressed the brakes that she'd already eased on then pulled onto the grass, away from the road for safety reasons. She sat there. She wanted to lay her forehead on her two hands that were gripping the steering wheel, the tightness ringing through her. Instead she sat there staring ahead and waited.

"I don't *ever* want to see that again," Jake declared in a gruff voice as he yanked the door open, reached down, and she realized she hadn't put on her seatbelt as he took her arm and pulled her from that car.

He pulled her straight into his embrace and hugged her tight. He trembled against her as he held her and her heart calmed against *his* raging heart. She leaned her head back and looked at him and saw fear in his eyes.

"I could have lost you," he said and then he dipped his head to hers and he kissed her.

* * *

Jake had been horrified watching Lara storm out of the

diner like a fire engine racing to a fire. He'd jumped up, but obviously when she stormed out that door then she'd raced to her car on her long legs. She'd just spun out of the parking lot as he'd jumped off the porch.

He raced to his SUV as her car on the road went from zero to who knows what in mere seconds! In that moment, in just a few seconds his heart had blown up as he raced to his vehicle. In seconds *he* was inside, then racing after her.

It didn't take long at the speed he was going to catch her, he was startled that she wasn't speeding, if she had been he might not have caught up to her. But she was intense and doing the speed limit of sixty-five, steady on the road. She wasn't zigzagging or wavering so in his mind she was hopefully concentrating, but in his mind and heart he was thankful she was okay and she pulled over. But she looked so stricken.

He hadn't been able to not kiss her. Feeling her in his arms, her lips on his, her heart pounding against his... He loved her, no denying it, he loved her with everything in him. If he had her for an instant before he let her go he had to take it all in. Absorb the feeling while he had it because she didn't want to love him.

She had lost more than her dad, she'd lost both of her parents. Her heart hurt and he understood it.

He made himself stop kissing her. Stop squeezing her, realizing then that she'd been kissing him too. He rested his forehead against hers. "I thought I had lost you. I'm so sorry. I didn't mean to kiss you. I've been trying not to let emotions overtake me. I am the sheriff. I'm a man of strength just like my dad."

She sighed. "Jake, we're both off course. That kiss...Jake," she breathed hard and then in a trembling voice she said, "I feel what my parents must have felt for each other." She looked up at him tears streaming down her eyes. "As much as I don't want to...they loved each other so much and they were together when that plane went down. My dad told me one time that he loved my mother so much that he didn't ever want to lose her. She told me the same thing about my dad. Neither of them wanted to lose the other one first. They wanted the other to live on, and celebrate life even without them." Her eyes brimmed with tears. "They loved each other so much and each wanted the other to live the longer life.

And enjoy life after losing the other. They wanted most to live a long life together to watch me give them grandchildren." She closed her beautiful eyes and took a breath.

Oh, how he loved her. "You were deeply loved."

"I was. And so were you. *Are*. Your mother loves you desperately. And my parents didn't want to die but they did together. Who knows what life holds? All I know is I—"

His heart thundered. "What?" he asked. He loved her. He loved her with every ounce of his soul. She said nothing. "I now know why mother is so afraid for me to find love. Because she knows how hard it hurts. But, I love you, Lara. I can't deny it and the guys were right. They told me I wasn't doing my job because I was distracted by my love for you. If love is going to distract me then I need to back down. I need to take my badge off and go for the love. And they're right. Absolutely right."

"You love me?"

He cupped her face with his hands, and gave her a soft, then firm kiss. "I love you. No denying it, and I believe you love me."

"I do. I don't want to."

His heart hurt and then she smiled and his heart danced.

"I don't want to but I do and there is no denying it and my parents taught me to embrace those I love. Like they embraced each other, and me and life. I love you, Jake Morgan. I love you with all of my heart and I cannot deny it. God is so good to give us this."

His heart pounded with joy. He swept her up into his arms and he spun, there on the side of the road in the grass like a man who loved a woman with all of his heart.

And that was him.

EPILOGUE

On the pier of the large lake, Jake and his bride stood along with the pastor who had just finished tying them together with "You are now husband and wife and you may kiss your bride." Thundering claps erupted from all the wonderful folks standing on the grass before the pier.

"Lara Morgan," Jake said softly as he took his bride into his arms, she smiled that smile that sent fireworks blasting through him and peace at the same time. "I do love the sound of that name. And I love the woman who goes with it even more."

Lara's eyes glistened. "I love being Mrs. Morgan. I'm thankful to our dear Lord that He led me here to Wishing Springs where I received the wish that I didn't know I was missing out on." She leaned closer, her arms tight around him as she looked up at him. "Kiss me, Mr. Morgan, and let's get this life started together."

His heart thundering in agreement, he dipped his head and their lips met...sweetness and dreams filled him. He could kiss Lara forever and he prayed they'd have a solid lifetime together. But one thing he knew was he was forever thankful she'd come looking for a new start in life and she'd ended up here in his arms and in his heart.

Cheers continued and he smiled against her lips as she did the same. Then they pulled apart and looked at the crowd watching them. He took Lara's hand and they walked toward everyone waiting to give them hugs and then get the party started.

Especially the smiling lady standing at the front of everyone, his sweet mother, her eyes glowed with tears of happiness for them. Her presence gave this special day an even happier ending. He and Lara were going to bless her with grandchildren...as many as Lara wanted—he was in for the calling. And he planned to fish on this pier with them with his dad in his heart.

Life was full of problems, small and large. But looking around at the town he'd vowed to watch over, he knew that the woman standing in his arms was his gift from God.

His heart thundered as the music played and they walked down the pier hand in hand...heart to heart forever. This was the beginning of a new life together and in that moment the eagle took everyone's attention as the majestic bird swooped from the blue sky, it's wings wide as it flew over them, did a graceful circle then flew back up into the sky.

Lara sighed then smiled at him. "I think that was your dad and my parents in spirit giving us a high five."

He pulled her back into his arms. "Darlin, this is a perfect day." Then she kissed him and he was home.

About the Author

Debra Clopton is a USA Today bestselling & International bestselling author who has sold over 3.5 million books. She has published over 81 books under her name and her pen name of Hope Moore.

Under both names she writes clean & wholesome and inspirational, small town romances, especially with cowboys but also loves to sweep readers away with romances set on beautiful beaches surrounded by topaz water and romantic sunsets.

Her books now sell worldwide and are regulars on the Bestseller list in the United States and around the world. Debra is a multiple award-winning author, but of all her awards, it is her reader's praise she values most. If she can make someone smile and forget their worries for a few hours (or days when binge reading one of her series) then she's done her job and her heart is happy. She really loves hearing she kept a reader from doing the dishes or sleeping!

A sixth-generation Texan, Debra lives on a ranch in Texas with her husband surrounded by cattle, deer, very busy squirrels and hole digging wild hogs. She enjoys traveling and spending time with her family.

Visit Debra's website and sign up for her newsletter for updates at: www.debraclopton.com

Check out her Facebook at:
www.facebook.com/debra.clopton.5

Follow her on Instagram at: debraclopton_author

or contact her at debraclopton@ymail.com

Made in the USA
Coppell, TX
09 August 2024

35790969R00134